THE
MISSING

THE
MISSING

CAROLINE ERIKSSON

TRANSLATED BY
TIINA NUNNALLY

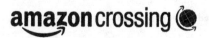

This is a work of fiction. Names, characters, organizations, places, events, and incidents are either products of the author's imagination or are used fictitiously.

Text copyright © 2015 Caroline Eriksson
Translation copyright © 2017 Tiina Nunnally
All rights reserved.

No part of this book may be reproduced, or stored in a retrieval system, or transmitted in any form or by any means, electronic, mechanical, photocopying, recording, or otherwise, without express written permission of the publisher.

Previously published as *De försvunna* by Bonnier in 2015 in Sweden. Translated from Swedish by Tiina Nunnally. First published in English by AmazonCrossing in 2016.

Published by AmazonCrossing, Seattle

www.apub.com

Amazon, the Amazon logo, and AmazonCrossing are trademarks of Amazon.com, Inc., or its affiliates.

ISBN-13: 9781503940659
ISBN-10: 1503940659

Cover design by David Drummond

Printed in the United States of America

To my maternal grandmother and grandfather:
For the summers at the cabin
For the pancakes and meatballs
For your wholehearted support of my writing
And for everything else

1

The little motorboat slices through the water with the precision of a knife. The sun is low in the sky; it's getting late on this evening at the end of summer. I'm sitting in the bow, closing my eyes to the water spraying up into my face, fighting against the nausea that churns inside my body and matches the movement of the boat. *If only he would slow down a little,* I think. And as if he has read my mind, that's exactly what Alex does. I turn around to face him. He's sitting in the stern with one hand on the tiller of the outboard motor. His whole being emanates masculinity and control. His shaved head, his clenched jaw, the furrow of concentration on his brow. Men aren't usually described as beautiful, but that's what Alex is. I've always thought so. And I still do.

Without warning, he shuts off the motor. The boat swerves in a small arc and then sinks back into the water. Smilla sways as she sits on the thwart between us. I lean forward and put my arms around her, holding on until she regains her balance. Instinctively she grabs hold of my hand with her little fingers, and a wave of warmth surges inside me. Now that the growl of the motor no longer fills the air, there is only silence. Smilla's fine, flaxen hair curls at the nape of her neck, less than an inch from my face. I'm just about to lean forward and bury my nose in the soft strands when Alex reaches for the oars.

"Do you want to try?"

Smilla instantly lets go of me and springs up.

"Come on, then," says Alex with a smile. "Papa's going to show you how to row."

He holds out his hand to her, helping her take the few steps to the stern. Once safely there, she sits down on his lap and happily pats him on the knee. Alex shows her how to hold the oars, and they slowly begin to row together. Smilla laughs, gurgling with delight the way only she can. I stare at the little dimples on her left cheek until my vision blurs. Then I turn to look out at the lake, losing myself in its expanse.

Alex claims the lake "probably has an official name in some public record," but around here no one calls it anything but "Malice." That's not all he says. He also tells stories, each one more gruesome than the last, about the lake and what locals say it's capable of doing. Tales warning that the waters have long been cursed and that their evil can seep into people, twisting their souls and making them commit horrific deeds. Children and adults alike have disappeared without a trace. Blood has been spilled. According to legend, that is.

An uncanny, plaintive sound echoes across the water, interrupting my thoughts. I turn toward it and notice out of the corner of my eye that Alex and Smilla have done the same. We hear it again. A low, throaty sound that rises to a hoarse, hooting shriek. A fluttering and then a dark shadow hurtles toward the surface of the lake a short distance away. The next instant, it's gone without the slightest splash or ripple, seemingly swallowed up by the water. Alex puts one arm around Smilla, stretching out his other hand to point.

"A loon," he explains. "Sometimes thought to be a prehistoric bird. Probably because of the sound it makes. A lot of people think it's scary."

He turns toward me, but I'm looking at Smilla and refuse to meet his eye. For a long moment, Smilla stares hard at the spot where the loon disappeared. Finally, she turns to Alex to ask him worriedly whether the bird is ever going to come up to breathe. He laughs, strokes her hair, and tells her the loon can stay underwater for several minutes. She shouldn't worry. "Besides," he adds, "it rarely comes up in the same place where it disappeared."

Alex picks up the oars to resume rowing the rest of the way. Smilla goes back to the middle of the boat to sit down, this time turned away from me. I study her profile from an oblique angle, seeing the soft curve of her cheek as she keeps searching the surface of the lake. The bird. She can't stop thinking about the bird, wondering where it is now and whether it can really survive so long underwater. I lift my hand, wanting to stroke her thin back to reassure her. At that moment, Smilla shifts position so I can no longer see her face. Alex is smiling at her, and I understand that she's smiling back. Trusting him. Relying on him. If Papa says the bird will be okay, then it will.

There are only about thirty feet to the island now. The small island in the middle of Lake Malice. That's where we're headed. I look down into the water, trying to pierce the surface with my eyes. With some effort, I can make out the bottom below us, overgrown with swaying reeds. The water is getting shallower. Algae floats upward, wrapping around the hull like long, slimy green fingers. Tall reeds rise up next to the boat and bend over our heads. When we run aground, Alex stands up and climbs past Smilla and me. His movements make the boat rock beneath us. I grip the gunwale and close my eyes until it stops.

Alex loops a mooring line around the nearest tree trunk and carefully ties it tight. Then he holds out his hand, and Smilla unsnaps her life vest as she totters past me. In her hurry, she manages to step on my foot and jab her elbow into my right breast. I yelp loudly, but she doesn't notice. Or if she does, she doesn't care. She's so eager to get to her father that nothing else matters. Anyone who sees them together can tell that Smilla loves Alex more than anything in the world. When we left the cabin and headed for the dock, she insisted on walking, or rather skipping, next to him. The slanting rays of the sun broke through the spruce branches along the narrow forest path; Smilla was happily chattering. Soon she and Papa would be going ashore on a desert island! Just like real pirates. Smilla was the pirate princess, and Papa could be . . . maybe the pirate king? Smilla laughed and tugged at Alex's hand. She couldn't get to the lake fast enough, while I walked several paces behind.

Now I glance up at them as they stand next to each other. Smilla is leaning against Alex with her soft little arms wrapped around his leg. An unbreakable unit. Father and daughter. The two of them on shore while I'm still sitting in the boat. This time, Alex holds out his hand to me, raising one eyebrow. I hesitate, and he notices.

"Come on. This is supposed to be a family outing, sweetheart."

He grins. My gaze shifts to Smilla, and our eyes meet. There's something about the way she's jutting out her little chin.

"You two go ahead," I say brusquely. "I'll wait here."

Alex makes one more halfhearted attempt to get me to come, but when I shake my head again, he shrugs and turns to Smilla. He makes a silly face, and her eyes shine with excitement.

"Watch out, everybody on the island! Here come Papa Pirate and Smilla, the pirate princess!" Alex shouts.

As Alex shouts these words, he picks up Smilla, throws her over his shoulder, and starts running up the slope. One side of the island is steeper than the other, and that's where we've come ashore. But Alex refuses to let the incline slow him down. I can almost feel the lactic acid in his legs. And the dizzy feeling in Smilla's tummy as she hangs upside down. Then they reach the top of the hill and disappear from view.

I sit and listen as the sound of their voices slowly fades away. After a while, I lean forward and gently massage the small of my back, which feels tender and stiff. Something makes me bend even farther forward to look over the side. The water is now almost motionless under the boat; the lake has closed up before my eyes. I can no longer see what's below the surface. The only thing staring back at me is my own splintered reflection. Finally, I allow the thoughts to come, the thoughts of what happened last evening and during the night. I go over every word, every movement as I keep staring at the reflection of my own eyes floating below me. With every remembered fragment, my stare seems to grow darker down there in the water. Involuntarily, I reach up and wrap my hands around my neck. A moment passes. Several minutes. An eternity.

Then I blink, and it's as if I'm waking up from a stupor, as if I'd lost all sense of time. How long have I been sitting here? I shiver and wrap my arms around myself. The sun is sinking below the treetops, sending bloodred streaks across the sky. A chill evening breeze sweeps in, and now I'm really feeling cold. I stretch my back and listen for any sounds, but I can no longer hear Alex's bellowing voice or Smilla's cheerful giggling. The only sound is the loon's desolate call, now from a distance. I shudder. Shouldn't they be done playing their pirate game and exploring the island by now? But then I think about how excited Smilla was. She probably won't be ready to give up this adventure any time soon. They're probably walking all around the island. Maybe they're playing hide-and-seek on the other side at this very moment. Maybe that's why I can't hear them anymore.

I close my eyes and think about how they roughhoused with each other in the kitchen this morning. I think about Alex's energy and his patience, which allow him to keep playing for such a long time. Long after other fathers would have grown tired. *Come on, honey, let's go back to the boat. Mama's waiting.* Alex would never say that. He's a good father. I open my eyes. Again I lean over the side and feel my gaze drawn to the darkening surface of the water.

Good father.
Good father.

Good father.

When I straighten up, there's still not a sound. No voices, no laughter. Not even a loon. I sit there for a while, not moving, just listening. Then, suddenly, I know. There's no need to take an anxious walk around the island, no need to go searching or to desperately shout their names. I don't even have to stand up and get out of the boat to know.

Alex and Smilla are not coming back. They're gone.

2

Of course I go look for them, in spite of my conviction that it won't do any good. Alex's dark-blue sweatshirt is folded up and lying in the stern. I grab it and stand up to pull the boat in. Uneasiness slithers down my spine. With a clumsy movement that's halfway between a step and a jump, I go ashore. I shout Alex's name, then Smilla's. No answer. My arms feel stiff as I pull the sweatshirt over my head. The fabric has a masculine scent that envelops me. It smells like Alex.

I feel a sharp stab in my gut but ignore the pain and start heading up the slope. I haven't gone more than a few steps when my chest tightens and I'm breathing hard. It's steeper than I thought. My body feels heavy and sluggish, refusing to cooperate, but I grit my teeth and force myself to continue, climbing upward. My foot slips in a muddy patch, and I have to put out my hand to keep from falling and sliding backward down the hill.

Finally I manage to reach the top. I try shouting again but can muster only a hoarse croak. My throat burns, protesting the strain, and my chest feels two sizes too small. Even though I make a great effort, my lungs are unable to supply the air that's needed. It feels like I'm trying to scream in the middle of a nightmare. My stomach cramps convulsively, wave after wave. I make another attempt to yell, but my body doubles over. Bending down, I emit a loud belch and then a dirty yellow sludge comes pouring out of me. My legs tremble and I totter to one side, then the other before dropping to my knees.

I wipe my mouth on the sleeve of the sweatshirt. I stay on the ground for a moment, as if felled by some superior foe. I push the thought away. *Foe? Superior? No!* I get back on my feet. My body still feels weak, but at least it's obeying. Instead of trying to shout again, I focus on surveying the island. There aren't many open spaces. Between scattered leafy trees and juniper bushes, I see waist-high grass and underbrush. There's no place that would allow easy passage. Especially for a four-year-old girl. I don't see Alex and Smilla anywhere.

I stumble forward, knowing what I have to do, but not sure which way to go. In one spot the grass has been pushed aside, and the ground looks trampled. So I head in that direction, following what I imagine are the tracks of a man and a little girl eager to play. Once in a while I pause to call their names, though not really expecting an answer. A perfunctory feeling comes over me, as if I'm acting in accordance with some preordained plan. I'm simply behaving the way I know I ought to behave, doing what I have to do. As if I'm playing a role.

The silence hovers, heavy and ominous, among the trees until, suddenly, there's a rustling in the grass just a few feet away. I flinch and instinctively clench my fists. Then I catch sight of a hedgehog scurrying away as fast as its little legs can go. When I look up again, the grass in front of me no longer shows any sign of being pushed aside or trampled. There's no indication that a man and a little girl have gone this way. I spin around to look behind me. Then forward again. And off to the sides. But there's no trace of people having passed this way, or even of my own path. I'm standing in a sea of tall grass. Silent and motionless, it surrounds me on all sides.

A wave of dizziness crashes over me, and I cover my eyes and stretch out one arm to keep my balance. Just as I take my hand away from my face and open my eyes, the last scarlet rays of the sun sink behind the treetops across the lake. I'm alone in an unfamiliar place, alone with the silence and the darkness that is now rapidly descending. I choose a direction at random and start moving through the inhospitable terrain.

A man and a little girl go ashore on a small island and don't come back. What could have happened? I tell myself there could be any number of plausible explanations. Maybe they got caught up in a game and forgot all about the time, or maybe they simply . . . Frantically I try to come up with other possible scenarios. Perfectly natural reasons. Innocent and benign. But the problem is that none of them can explain why Alex and Smilla are still missing, and why they don't respond to my calls. I open my mouth to shout again, and I'm shocked at the hysteria I hear in my own voice.

As I stumble onward, I train my eyes on the ground and the trees. My feet move faster, and my movements become more disjointed. I proceed aimlessly, no longer aware in which direction I'm going or where I've come from. I'm so stressed that I can't orient myself properly. Nowhere do I see any trace of human life. A sob rises from my chest. *Smilla!*

At that instant, I catch sight of something. I stop, noticing a trembling that spreads through my whole body. I see a rock a couple of yards up ahead. And then, a short distance from there, something else. A dark object. Even though I don't immediately understand what I'm looking at, I know with every fiber of my being it's not part of the vegetation. It belongs to a person. Slowly, filled with dread at what I might find, I approach and crouch down in the grass. It's a single black shoe, tattered and worn. The tiny holes that once held shoelaces now gape. The tension in my chest eases a bit: I've never seen this shoe before. It doesn't belong to Alex or Smilla. That much I know. Not understanding why, I hold out my hand, sensing how it's slowly but surely being sucked down toward the shoe. As if my fingers are being controlled by some outside force, a force rising up from the ground beneath my feet.

With a gasp, I jerk my hand back and stand up. What are these strange ideas and notions that keep creeping into my mind? Remnants of Alex's ghost stories must be lingering in my consciousness. The stories about Lake Malice and its malevolent powers. Briskly I continue on, reminding myself that those tales are nothing more than supernatural nonsense mixed with old superstitions. Yet I can't help looking over my shoulder several times. My feet cut through the grass faster and faster until I'm practically jogging.

I weave between the tree trunks, their shadows growing deeper, their scraggly branches reaching for me like long, malevolent arms. Something grabs hold of me, twigs scrape at my scalp like claws, and I scream loudly, unable to stop myself. The sound of my own terror is too much for me. Thoughts spring into my mind and race wildly, no longer under my control, whipping up greater and greater waves of emotion inside me. *I'm not going to find them. I'm never going to find them.*

But then—at that very moment—something occurs to me. *Make a phone call.* If I can't find them, I need to call. Of course. That's the first thing to do when someone goes missing. Why didn't I think of that before? I slow down and, breathing hard, shove my hand in the pocket of my capris. Empty. I check the other pocket, but my cell phone isn't there either. Where could it be? Did I lose it somewhere on the island? Or did I leave it back in the boat? Fragments of memory slowly coalesce.

I didn't take my cell with me when we left the cabin. It was an impulsive decision to set off on this excursion, and I actually hadn't intended to go along. Yet I did. My chest tightens again, but this time it's not from straining to breathe. Again I look around, desperately trying to see a tiny scrap of pale-pink fabric, a flutter of blond hair. But she's no longer here. I know that. I can feel it. I left my phone back at the cabin, probably in my purse. There's only one thing to do.

Yet it doesn't feel right. How can I leave the island without having found Alex and Smilla? How can I simply leave them to their fate? *To their fate . . .* There's something terrible about those words. *This doesn't make sense. Something is wrong. Very wrong.*

No! I push away the sinister whispering inside me and start walking faster. Once I get hold of my phone, everything will work out. I'll be able to call Alex, or he'll call me. Who knows, maybe he has already tried to reach me. I pick up the pace even more, ignoring how exhausted I feel. I need to get my hands on my phone ASAP. The only question is whether I'll be able to find my way back to the spot where we tied up the boat.

I take another step forward and I'm falling into the dark. The ground disappears from beneath me. At the last second I manage to stay on my feet, but my stomach lurches. When I calm down, I stand still for a long time, staring at the sight in front of me. It's the hill I came up. The hill that, from this direction, is more like a treacherous precipice. How could I be back here already? In my confused state I could hardly tell which way I'd been heading. But here it is. Below I can see the outline of the boat, rocking among the reeds as if nothing has happened. I stare at it with mixed emotions. Clearly Alex and Smilla aren't down there waiting for me, but at least the boat is still there. The next second it occurs to me what a strange thought that is. Why wouldn't the boat be there?

Something is nagging at me. A certain uneasiness. Or is it regret? *If I could turn back time, do things differently, undo what was done . . .* I shake off the feeling and once again glance over my shoulder. It's dark now, everything immersed in shadow. I picture two silhouettes, one tall and one short, emerging from the dim light and rushing toward me with loud shouts and laughter. But no one is there. No one's coming.

A bird flutters past, so close that I think I can feel the rushing of its wings. I glimpse the contours of a sleek body and a dagger-shaped beak. The loon dives for the water. For a moment I stare after it. Then I step over the edge.

3

Somehow I manage to make my way back. I get the boat moving and go as fast as I can away from the island and across the lake to the slightly rickety dock. A large number of skiffs and small fiberglass boats are already there, bobbing at their moorings, but all of them are empty. My hands are shaking and I can hardly make my fingers obey as I tie up the boat. My body feels stiff and tense and I'm breathing hard as I stumble up the narrow path leading away from the lake. A tree root sticking out of the ground makes me lose my balance and trip. The old pain in my thigh flares up, but I grit my teeth and keep going, keep climbing. The cabin is silently waiting, the last in the row of houses on the road. It's protected from view by a hedge of arborvitae on one side and a steep mountain wall on the other. The key is right where we left it, under the front steps.

My fingers are ice cold as I fumble with the key. I have to take several deep breaths before I succeed in unlocking the door. Just as I'm about to close the door behind me, I see a furry creature slink past my legs and into the cabin. I hear a furious meowing, as if Tirith has been waiting ages to come inside and wants to tell me how indignant he is at such neglect. Paying no attention to the cat and not bothering to take off my shoes, I rush inside to turn on the lights and check all the rooms, yelling as I go. I shout for Alex and Smilla, but no one answers. The cabin looks exactly the same as it did when we left. As if time has stood still inside while we've been gone. In the kitchen I see a pile of newspapers on the table, next to a dirty yogurt bowl. Smilla's Barbie dolls are scattered across the floor. When I think about how she was sitting in this very spot, playing with the dolls earlier in the day, the tight feeling in my chest gets worse.

Then I notice the mark on the floor. A single footprint. Dark and sticky, with a clear impression from the sole of a shoe. *Did someone break into the cabin while we were gone? Has somebody been inside? Is it . . . ?* I look up and feel the hairs rise on the back of my neck and along my forearms. *Is someone here right now? Is somebody hiding under a bed or in a wardrobe, just waiting to attack me?* An icy shiver races through me. Then I notice another footprint, and another. They're all coming from the same direction. From me.

I look down at my feet and catch sight of my pink sneakers—the shoes that I was in too much of a hurry to take off when I came inside. One shoe is still more or less decent-looking, but the other one is covered with brown splotches. I lift my foot and see how dirty the sole is. When I tentatively sniff at the air, a clammy smell fills my nostrils. Mud. I must have stepped in it somewhere. Then I remember slipping in something as I climbed the slope. Could it be mud from the island that is now tracked across the cabin floor? Mud from that island, the island where Alex and Smilla . . . Again I run my eyes over the footprints, as nausea takes hold. How could I leave the island without them?

A movement in the room catches my attention. Tirith is standing in front of me. The fur on his neck fluffs over the thin pink collar he's wearing. His tail swings slowly from side to side as he stares at me, his eyes narrowed. As if he's wondering what I'm doing here, alone, wearing a sweatshirt that belongs to his master. We stare at each other. The cat's yellow eyes shift to look at the footprints on the floor and then back up at me. I imagine that he's demanding an explanation. *What do you mean, missing? How could they just disappear?* I bury my head in my hands, stifling a scream. Thoughts whirl through my mind, sucking me into a perilous maelstrom.

Somehow I manage to get hold of myself. I picture myself from a distance, standing there, doing nothing, a defeated and pitiful figure in every way. *Get a grip on yourself this minute!*

"I have to call Alex," I say out loud, taking my hands away from my face. "That's why I came back."

I feel like I'm explaining things to both the cat and myself. The words—spoken firmly and clearly—are my defense against the silent and treacherous thoughts. Those thoughts are not trustworthy. If I allow them to take charge I'll end up plunging into the dark. If I look up and try to take in the whole picture, fear will paralyze me. It's important to look at one detail at a time, to focus on one thing at a time. That's the only way I can hold on to my sanity.

There's no landline in the cabin, so the first thing I need to do is find my cell phone. I take off my shoes and carry them back to the front entryway. Wiping up the floor will have to wait. Resolutely I head for the bedroom at the end of the hall.

The room that belongs to Alex and me is dominated by a big double bed. My heart lurches when I think about the last time we were in that bed together. With an effort I manage to quell the dizziness and calm the anxious fluttering in my stomach.

Everything is nice and tidy on Alex's side of the room. His clothes are hanging in the wardrobe or neatly folded and stowed in the dresser drawers. He has even made the bed on his side. The side where he usually sleeps. Where he slept last night. But where is he now? My side of the mattress is covered with summer dresses, jeans, and tops. My purse is on the bedside chair along with a pile of paperbacks and two lipsticks. Draped over the back is my lacy red bra, the one I bought when we decided to go on this trip. That was the same day I bought Alex the black silk tie. I swallow hard, an almost reflexive action. *Don't think about that now. Don't think at all. Just focus on doing what has to be done.*

Quickly I rummage through my purse, turning all the pockets inside out, and finally turning the whole thing upside down. But no cell phone falls out. *How strange. Where could it be?* I hurry back to the kitchen. Tirith darts past, heading for his bowl, hoping I'll feed him. He circles it a few times, then sits down in disappointment and licks his lips.

"Everything's going to be fine, I just have to find . . ."

I keep chattering—mostly to calm myself down—as I rush around the kitchen, sweeping the newspapers aside and moving the dirty dishes on the table. I check under Smilla's Barbie dolls, behind the coffeemaker, and on the shelf above the stove. No cell phone. I even open the fridge and scan the shelves inside before heading to the living room.

As I search the room, I imagine what I'll say to Alex. What our conversation might be like. And how he'll laugh when I call him.

You'll never guess what happened!

I can almost hear him telling me how he and Smilla disappeared. Giving me an absurd and yet completely natural explanation. Because there must be some explanation, there has to be. The only problem is that right now I can't for the life of me imagine what it might be. *This is crazy.* That's the thought that crosses my mind as I run my hands over the springs under the sofa cushions. They're gone. But it's not possible to simply disappear like that. Not from an island.

I tear open the curtains to look on all the windowsills. In my hurry I knock over a little glass figurine. I see it tumble through the air as if in slow motion, hit the floor, and shatter into a thousand pieces. The rational and focused approach that I've fought so hard to maintain slowly slips away. Desperation is nipping at me from all sides. A shrill ringing in my ears propels me back to the bedroom. Again I rummage through my purse but find nothing. Feverishly I toss aside the clothes on the bed, along with the books and the lipsticks on the chair. My phone's not there.

So I run over to Smilla's room and ransack all her belongings too. Dolls and teddy bears, activity books, and stickers. I move fast, my actions bordering on manic. I know that I'm looking for something, but by now I've forgotten what it is. All I can think about is Smilla. Sweet little Smilla. My thoughts are whirling, running wild. I lose control and feel myself drawn helplessly down into the vortex I was fighting to avoid. *Missing. They're missing.* But that's impossible! A grown man and a four-year-old girl can't just get swallowed up by the earth.

No, not by the earth, but by the lake, by the water that is laced with evil.

People have disappeared, blood has been spilled. Alex's words echo in my head, panic races up my spine.

Out of the corner of my eye I see something move, followed by a loud bang. I spin on my heel and yell. The sound of hundreds of tiny beads rolling across the floor fills my ears, and at the same moment I catch sight of Tirith. My shout makes him freeze midstride. He looks both alarmed and guilty. As silence returns to the room, his gaze shifts from me to the jar of beads that has toppled over. He must have followed me in here, padding soundlessly into the room. Maybe he mistook my search for some sort of game and wanted to play too. Maybe he knocked Smilla's jar of beads off the shelf by accident.

I fan out the fingers of one hand and press them to my chest as I take several deep breaths. Then I reach out my other hand toward the cat. After a brief hesitation, he approaches. I stroke his back slowly, steadily. An attempt to calm both of us. He rubs against me, and on impulse I pick him up in my arms, pressing his warm body close. Hot tears fill my eyes, and my vision blurs. A sob rises in my throat and spills from my lips.

"She'll come back," I whisper. "You'll see. She'll be back soon."

I can hear how phony those words sound. And it's obvious I don't believe them myself. Does the cat notice too? I bury my face in Tirith's fur and hear him start to purr. When I lift my head, he narrows his eyes and pokes his nose toward me. Then he licks my cheeks, running his rough tongue over my face. As if he wants to console and encourage me. We sit like that for a while until he slips out of my grasp and onto the floor, where he begins grooming himself. I get up and go back to the living room, my hands clenched at my sides. Where is that damn cell phone? I need to find it now! If only I could get hold of Alex, everything would be fine. *Not if,* I instantly correct myself. *When. When* I get hold of him.

I search the living room again, looking in every conceivable spot, every nook and cranny, both around and underneath all the furniture. But the phone seems to have vanished into thin air. My pulse is pounding in my ears. All I want to do is scream hysterically. Then I hear a sound and freeze. A second passes, then I hear it again. The muted and distant but unmistakable sound of a phone ringing. My phone. It sounds like it's coming from the bedrooms. I run, or rather stumble, back down the hall, stopping outside the bedrooms. I stand still, my heart hammering, and listen for the next ring. *Don't let it switch to voice mail! I can't let that happen!*

It rings again, clearly coming from the bedroom I share with Alex, from the bed itself. I rush inside. Strangely enough, the sound is coming from Alex's side. I grab the duvet he spread so neatly and yank it off. I'm staring at an object lying on top of the smooth white sheet. My cell phone. Hidden under the duvet on Alex's fastidiously neat side of the bed.

I can't understand how it ended up there, but I can't waste any more time thinking about that. The phone lights up and rings again. Fumbling, I pick up the phone and stare at the display. An all-too-familiar number. *Not now!* I don't know why I take the call. All I know is that, as I answer, I shut my eyes tight.

4

It's my mother. She's breathing hard, and my stomach clenches with the constant, nagging dread from my childhood. Did something happen? It only lasts a moment. *That calamity has already occurred, it took place a long time ago.* There could be any number of reasons for Mama's rapid breathing. Maybe she just came in from her evening walk, although I don't know whether she's still fond of taking walks. And I don't care. I think about Alex. About the fact that by this time he might have left a message on my voice mail. Maybe he's trying to call me at this very second.

"Mama, I have to—"

But she doesn't seem to hear me. Undeterred, she starts talking, telling me how tired she is. She's had several extremely trying days. A client has threatened one of her colleagues.

"It was the usual sort of thing. 'I know where you live and where your children go to school.' Except this time the guy flipped her desk over."

I want to scream that I'm a grown-up now and I've got my own problems, that things are happening in my life that are way more frightening than what she's talking about. But of course I say nothing.

Mama pauses, murmurs, "Hmm," and then moves on to the next topic of conversation, the lovely late summer weather. Nausea rises inside me. Why does she do this? Stubbornly pretending that we're just an ordinary mother and daughter. As if it were possible for the two of us to truly communicate after all these years, to reach past what's between us and connect with each other again. *Reach past what happened. Papa, who disappeared.*

I sink down onto the bed, touch my forehead with my free hand. Mama falls silent, and I realize that she has asked me something. I clear my throat. I'm forced to ask her to repeat the question.

"Are you alone?"

A wave of emotions surges inside me. That question doesn't belong here. It belongs to the time before Alex. All those nights when I came home to an empty apartment to sit alone at the kitchen table, with the silence echoing off the walls and only a lit candle to keep me company. That intense longing for companionship and closeness. And the equally intense fear of letting anyone behind my protective walls. *Are you alone?*

Again I feel hot tears fill my eyes, and I shake my head in an attempt to hold them back. It's not like me to be so emotional, not at all. But I haven't been myself since my appointment at the clinic a couple of weeks ago. And after what happened last night, how could anything go on as usual? In my mind's eye, I picture Lake Malice, the calm and bewitched water of the lake. The island in the middle, the steep slope on one side, and the dark crowns of the trees etched against the sky. *Alex. Smilla.*

"Yes, I'm alone."

Mama sighs. *You're such a disappointment, Greta.* She doesn't say that, but I can tell it's what she's thinking. I swallow the lump in my throat, pull myself together.

"Mama, I can't . . . I really need to—"

"You sound different. Has something happened?"

What if I told her the situation? What if I told her everything? What would happen then? Would she jump into the car and drive right over and sweep me up in her arms? Would she take charge of everything just like she did my whole childhood? Push me onto a chair and tell me how things are going to be done from now on? What has to be done, what I should say, think, and feel? Probably.

"It's so quiet on your end," Mama goes on, and now she suddenly sounds like she's on the alert. "Where exactly are you?"

I take a deep breath. Then I end the call. When the phone rings again and the same number appears on the display, I switch off the ringer.

5

On unsteady legs, I leave the bedroom. Not that the conversations I have with my mother are ever very relaxing, but this one bothers me more than usual. Those mundane words we spoke, those banal phrases. All of it such a glaring contrast to the confusing, nightmarish circumstances in which I find myself.

I pause halfway between the living room and kitchen, feeling my phone vibrate for the third time. *How long is it going to take for her to give up?* Tirith, who's lying on the sofa, raises his head to give me a demanding look.

"I will, I will," I murmur.

I have no idea what I mean by that. Something has to be done, but what? The conversation with my mother knocked me off balance. I need to back up, start over. Didn't I have some sort of plan? First find the phone, and then . . . then what? What should I do now?

I stare at the hard object in my hand. It was on Alex's side of the bed the whole time. Stuffed under the duvet, tucked away. Like someone put it there on purpose. Hid it. *No!* I shake my head, dismissing the vague notion taking shape. How and why my cell ended up there is irrelevant. The only thing that matters is now I can connect with the outside world. Now I can call Alex. *Yes, of course. That's what I need to do.*

With trembling fingers, I punch in the number and wait. The sound of his voice makes my throat close up. For a fraction of a second I think I'm actually listening to Alex speaking on the phone. And this whole thing is over. But then I realize it's just his voice mail. I hit the "End" button and try again. Listen again to the rapid-fire words spoken in Alex's professional-salesman voice. I call four or five times. Each time, I get the same recording. And when the beep tells me it's time to leave my own message, I say nothing. I have no idea what to say. What are the right words when all you want is an explanation for something inexplicable?

"Hi, this is Alex . . ." The greeting sends me back in time, to our very first meeting.

He came into the shop with one of his colleagues. Katinka was the first to notice him.

"Hey, look," she whispered, giving me a poke in the side.

I turned around, and there he was. His suit was perfectly tailored, his head shaved. His white shirt was neatly pressed, but when he held out his hand, the cuff slid back to reveal intertwining tattoos on his forearm. There was something about the contrast that captivated me. He told us he was introducing a new line of beauty products promoted by a famous singer. His colleague may have said something too, but if so, I was only vaguely aware of it. I recall a brief silence in which Alex fixed his steel-blue eyes on me.

"Greta? Is that your name?"

Just then, the shop owner showed up, greeting him with a polite smile and quick handshake. Apparently, they had an appointment. Alex gave us a nod and followed our boss to the small office at the other end of the shop. I was sure he could feel my eyes glued to his back. I thought he'd turn his head to smile at me, but he didn't.

The launch of the singer's beauty line turned out to involve an unusually elaborate and expensive promotion. Life-size cardboard cutouts depicting the singer in various glamorous poses were set up in the shop. Pink alcohol-free bubbly in tall glasses and fancy chocolate pralines were displayed on gilded trays. In front of an audience, Katinka and I showed customers how to apply the makeup. On one occasion I noticed Alex among the spectators crowded below the podium where I was standing. The look in his eyes sent a bolt of desire through me. The attraction was so strong I lost my voice. Afterward, when things settled down and we were cleaning up, he suddenly appeared at my side.

"Greta," he said. "Like Garbo."

Or Gretel, I thought. Mine was almost the same name as the girl in the fairy tale about the gingerbread house and the evil witch in the woods. But I didn't say that. I didn't manage to say a word. That was how strong an effect he had on me. A nod was all I could manage. He gave me a crooked grin.

"So your mother named you after a movie star?"

I cleared my throat. "Actually, it was my father who came up with the name."

I instantly regretted mentioning him. *Don't ask. Please don't ask.* But Alex didn't ask any questions about Papa. Not then. Instead, he leaned nonchalantly against a shelf of perfume bottles and took a sip from the glass he was holding.

"Well, it suits you, at any rate. Garbo was a real beauty."

He was staring at me with such intensity in his blue eyes that I had to look away. I straightened the black T-shirt with the shop logo I was wearing, keenly aware of his gaze following the movement of my hands on the fabric.

"And she was not only beautiful, she was also a mystery. I have a feeling that you are too."

◆　◆　◆

Something warm rubs against my leg and I look down, giving Tirith a distracted look. Only later did I tell Alex about Papa. And even then I didn't reveal the whole truth. *A mystery. I have a feeling that you are too.* Yes, well. Maybe.

I lean down to stroke the cat under the chin. With my other hand, I hold the phone to my ear. Tirith blissfully closes his eyes and leans his head against me, butting at my fingers. I check my own voice mail, but there's nothing from Alex. Again I punch in his number. This time I do leave a message. How would it look otherwise? That's what pops into my mind. The next second, I frown. *How would it look otherwise?* What a strange thought.

Restless, I wander into the kitchen. I find a rag and make a halfhearted attempt to wipe the mud off the floor. In the living room, I pick up all the pieces of the broken figurine. Wondering what to do next, I make another round of the cabin, entering one room after the other. In the entryway, I pause. I stand there for a long time, listening for any sounds outside, for footsteps coming up the steps and loud voices approaching. I'm waiting for someone to grab the door handle and call my name. Call out: *We're here!* But nothing happens. My mind feels both jumbled and completely empty. *Missing. Gone. It's impossible.*

I turn to look in the mirror that hangs on the wall across from the coat hooks and hat shelf. I study the dark-haired figure with carefully applied makeup. I take her in. Take in the whole picture. Except for the purplish shadow on her neck. My eyes move quickly past that. Then I look into my own eyes, trying to penetrate the barrier that separates me from the rest of the world. The barrier that has always been my protection. My weapon. What would other people do in my situation? What would an ordinary, sensible, normal person do now?

I know the answer even before those words take shape in my consciousness. *Call for help.* That's what an ordinary, sensible, normal person would do under these circumstances. How could I have let all these hours go by—and by now many hours must have passed— without sounding the alarm about Alex and Smilla's disappearance? Why don't I instantly pick up the phone and contact the police? My cheeks are burning as I tear myself away from the eyes, now looking even sterner, staring at me from the mirror. Calling the police would mean acknowledging the likelihood that something terrible has happened. The worst of all possible scenarios. And I refuse to think along those lines. Alex and Smilla are unharmed and safe. That's what I want to believe, what I need to believe. *But then why aren't they here? Here with you?* A shiver races down my spine, making the tiny hairs on my arms and the back of my neck stand on end. I need to go back to the island. I have to.

When I try to put on my shoes, I sway and almost fall over.

Only now do I realize how worn out I am. Totally exhausted. Before I leave I should probably sit down for a while. I can't eat anything, but I should at least drink something.

I stumble into the kitchen and run my hands over the cupboards above the sink but don't open any of them. Instead, I open the lower cupboard and survey the bottles stowed inside. What I really need is a drink. I slam the cupboard door and sink into a kitchen chair. I can't have a drink. Not now. Definitely not now.

The outline of a face hovers in front of me. I can make out a man's sharp features. Hair falling in a wave over his forehead, full lips curving in a strongly defined arch. Papa? Papa. It's too much. The last shreds of self-confidence and determination seep out of me. I bury my face in my hands and slump forward.

Damn you, Alex!

6

I wake up when something soft and furry presses against my face. I instinctively try to fend off consciousness as well as whatever is trying to force itself on me. When I automatically throw out my arm—*I won't let you, I don't want to*—I bump into a slender, warm body, prompting an offended yowl. In an instant, I'm wide awake. I raise my head. My neck is so stiff that I moan out loud; one side of my face has gone numb. I rub my cheek and stare down at the tablecloth. Did I fall asleep here?

Tirith has moved away and is now standing a safe distance away, giving me an accusatory look.

"Sorry, I didn't mean to," I say, wheezing slightly as I rub my tight neck. "I didn't know it was you. I thought . . ."

Then I remember. I haul myself to my feet and rush for the bedrooms. In Smilla's room, everything is a mess from yesterday's search. But I hardly notice. The only thing I see is the bed. Empty. No golden curls spread out on the pillow, no little girl's body outlined under the covers. I fall to my knees, bury my face in the duvet, and breathe in her scent. It can't be true. Maybe I'm still asleep? *Oh, dear God, please tell me I'm dreaming. Make all of this a bad dream.*

I can feel myself hovering on the verge of tears. A whimper rises to my throat and out of my mouth. But then something squeezes in between me and all these emotions. An ugly voice in my head. *Hypocrite,* it whispers. I stagger to my feet, my eyes dry. Dutifully, I peek inside the bigger bedroom—and conclude that no one has slept there either. My head feels heavy, as if I'd had that drink yesterday after all. I feel like I must've emptied, one by one, all those fucking bottles that Alex brought, even though I know this never happened. *How can you be so sure?* whispers the little voice inside my head. *How can you be sure of anything?*

Tirith is waiting in the kitchen. He eagerly swings his tail from side to side when I get out the bag of cat food and pour some in his dish. Of course that's why he woke me up. He's hungry. I had planned to take only a short nap, yet here it is already morning. Filled with loathing, I stick two pieces of French bread in the toaster. Out of habit I also fill a bowl with yogurt. I try to avoid thinking how absurd it is to be bothering with ordinary routines right now. I need food, after all, so I force myself to eat.

The toast crunches between my teeth, and my throat hurts when I swallow. Cautiously, I touch my neck. Then I run my eyes over the kitchen table, to the place where Smilla was sitting only twenty-four hours ago.

They came into the kitchen together. Alex with his arms stretched overhead, one hand supporting Smilla under her chest, the other holding on to her leg. She was swooping like an airplane over his head, howling with laughter when he spun around and made her do breakneck dives through the air. At one point, her head came dangerously close to an open cupboard door, and it looked like Alex might lose his balance. But I held back my objections, not wanting to fuss, not wanting to interfere.

Finally, Alex brought Smilla in for a landing on the chair across from me and began fixing her breakfast. She tucked her feet up under her nightgown and watched him with admiration in her eyes. Maybe it was Smilla's pure and genuine happiness that settled the matter. Maybe it was then that I solidified the decision I'd made during the night.

Good father.

Good father.

Good father.

I can still picture Smilla in front of me, but the features of her face seem distorted. As if she's sitting there on the kitchen chair across from me, and yet she isn't. Suddenly, it's myself that I see. And the man moving around the kitchen, the man in charge of games and roughhousing, is Papa. The man who only a moment ago set me down on the chair after letting me climb around, hang upside down, and spin in circles, safely held by his strong body and firm grip. The man who is now opening cupboards and drawers, ostensibly to make breakfast, but who can't stop goofing off, turning everything into a game. He balances a plate on my head and pretends to spread butter on a napkin instead of the toast. When he leans down to kiss my cheek, I smell morning breath from his mouth and women's perfume on his skin.

Mama comes in, still bleary with sleep and with her hair in disarray. She stifles a yawn with her hand, and Papa dances over to her, humming some sort of silly tune. She keeps her hand over her mouth, but I can still see that her face lights up with a crooked smile. *I have the world's craziest husband.* They give each other a long, passionate kiss, and when Papa thinks that I can't hear—or that I'm too little to understand—he murmurs: *Thanks for last night.* Mama laughs, embarrassed, and rolls her eyes. But she's happy. I see how her eyes are shining. And I feel happy and warm inside too. My parents love each other. And they love me. I have everything anyone could wish for.

I raise the spoon to my lips, my hand trembling slightly. That's a nice childhood memory, but it would have been even nicer if it were true.

If it hadn't been largely fabricated after the fact. If Mama had really been in a good mood when she came into the kitchen instead of being silent and morose. If the smell coming from Papa's mouth hadn't been the residue of the previous day's festivities. And if I could pretend that I didn't understand. I knew that the scent on his skin did belong to a woman, but the woman was not my mother.

The pieces of toast swell inside my mouth. I stare at the bread that I'm holding. Notice how my hand is shaking. My stomach clenches and churns. Yet it still takes a moment before I comprehend what's about to happen. When the realization takes hold, I jump up from the table so fast that my chair hits the floor with a bang. The next second my feet are pounding across the floor. Tirith shoots like a missile under the living room sofa. But I have no time to pay attention to a frightened cat. I yank open the bathroom door and hurl myself forward, managing to reach the toilet just in time before the vomit gushes out of my mouth.

7

A cloudless morning. Sunlight glinting off the shiny paint of the car, which is parked on the road outside the cabin. It's my car. The car we drove to get here. Now there it stands, its headlights like wide-open, empty eyes, and it seems to be mutely shouting at me. *Save yourself while you can, escape before it's too late.* But that's not a viable idea. It's impossible to flee from here. I can't leave Marhem until I've found Alex and Smilla.

I move a little closer, tilting my head to one side as I study the tracks in the gravel next to the car. The tracks left by another vehicle as it roared off with an angry lurch. Pensively, I follow the indentations until they straighten out and merge with the others on the road. I think about what happened the other night. About how I woke up, heard sounds from outside, and noticed that Alex wasn't in bed. A loud, agitated voice penetrated the window, which was slightly open. And then: the sharp slamming of a car door followed by screeching tires.

The sun is roasting hot, burning my forearms, but I stand still and keep staring at the tracks on the road. I think about that other car and the two people who were inside. About the one who stayed and the one who left. Finally, I turn my back on the tracks, not wanting to think anymore.

A while later, I find myself down at the dock, shading my eyes with my hand and staring at the lake, across its secretive, steel-gray surface.

Then I'm back in the boat, in the middle of Lake Malice, with the island in view. I put in at the same place as yesterday, then unsteadily make my way ashore, head up the slope, and take a look around. Not even twelve hours have passed since I last stood in this exact same spot, and there's no time to lose. With great determination, I set off. This time, I carry out my search in a more methodical manner. I cover the island bush by bush, one thicket after another. The black shoe is still lying where I found it last night, but this time I walk right past, refusing to be distracted.

The island is definitely less scary in daylight, but the terrain is just as difficult to traverse. Fallen trees and overgrown vegetation are mixed with patches of marsh and mud. My shoes are constantly sinking into brownish-black muck, and I have to fight to pull free. Alex and Smilla must have encountered the same trouble when they were exploring the island. It couldn't have been easy for Smilla, since the land is far from hospitable. In spite of her initial enthusiasm, she must have grown tired of the adventure very quickly. And yet she and Alex chose to continue their game instead of returning to me and the boat. Did something happen? If so, where have they gone? Did something prevent them from coming back? What could that be? I stop midstride. There is something inside of me that is protesting, resisting. Somehow, all my thoughts and the questions I'm asking seem spurious. Phony. Like I'm trying to fool myself.

I sit down on a tree stump, take out my cell, and call Alex. Mostly just for something to do, a way of distracting myself. He still doesn't pick up, and once again I listen to his polite and professional recorded greeting. I end the call. Maybe it would be best if I didn't try calling anymore. Every time I hear Alex's voice, it brings up so many things, painful things. I tuck my legs under me and my mind is instantly flooded with thoughts of how it all started.

It was a few days after the launch party for the new beauty products, maybe a week at most. I left work early and went out to the parking lot next to the shopping mall with my jacket open. Most of the snow had melted away, and the sun held the promise of approaching spring, but the wind was brisk, and there was still no warmth in the air. I noticed the dark car parked by the entrance but didn't pay it much attention until someone honked the horn and rolled down the passenger-side window. It was Alex. I automatically reached up to brush a few strands of hair out of my face. I went slowly to his car, placed my hand on the edge of the open window, and leaned down.

"What are you doing here?"

He laughed hoarsely, grinned, and asked if I'd had a bad day, or was I always so high and mighty? At first, I didn't understand. Then I blushed, realizing my question could be interpreted as arrogant rather than an expression of genuine surprise. Before I could explain or apologize, he went on.

"I've been waiting for you. You're the reason I'm here."

Because of me? Could that be true? But why? No matter how hard I tried, I couldn't say a word.

"I was thinking I could give you a ride home. Hop in."

He sounded so calm, so confident. As if it were the most natural thing in the world to offer me a lift, even though we didn't know each other at all. I raised my head to glance toward the bus stop. In a few minutes, my bus would leave, taking me home to the kitchen table, the silence. And the loneliness. Which protected me. And weighed on me.

"How did you know when I'd get off work?"

"I have my ways."

I think Alex finally leaned over and opened the car door for me, and that's why I got in. Because he made the decision for me. I'd hardly sat down and murmured my address before he leaned over. I felt the blood surge to my cheeks. Then I realized that I'd misunderstood. He was reaching for the seatbelt on the passenger side. With great care, he pulled it across my body and buckled me in. No one had ever done that for me as an adult. There was something so protective about the gesture. Such a show of old-fashioned chivalry. I liked it. A lot.

Alex put on his sunglasses, and we headed for the highway. Now and then, he'd turn to look at me. The crooked smile was gone and the mood had shifted to a more serious tone. I wanted to say something clever and interesting but could only come up with platitudes about the weather. My heart was pounding, and my mouth had gone dry. When at last we pulled up in front of my building, I gathered my courage and placed a hand gently on his arm.

"Thanks for the lift."

Alex didn't reply. Nor did he turn toward me. He didn't move at all except for a slight shrug. His hands still gripped the steering wheel, and he was staring straight ahead. As if steeling himself for something. Or— it occurred to me—as if he wanted to get away as fast as possible. Maybe he didn't like my perfume. Maybe I wasn't thin enough. Or maybe the short car ride had been sufficient to prove that my personality was anything but exciting.

I wanted to scream at myself.

How could I ever have thought that someone like me would be attractive to a man like him? Waves of heat washed over my face and through my body. No matter what I'd hoped or imagined, it was all an illusion. Of course. My hand shook as I fumbled for the door handle. I had to get out of this car. I had to get in my building and up to my apartment. To the emptiness and the silence.

"Please don't go."

His hand grabbed mine, holding me back. Slowly, I turned. Alex's face was now close to mine, so close that I could feel his warm breath against my cheeks when he opened his mouth to speak.

"There's something about you. I don't know what it is, but you make me want to . . . take care of you."

For some reason, probably because of the slight hesitation before he spoke those last words, I had the impression that he'd actually intended to say something else. I wanted to look into his eyes, but they were hidden behind dark sunglasses.

He ran two fingers lightly over my palm, and a thrill of pleasure raced up my forearm and through my body.

Alex let me go and gestured toward the backseat. I turned to see two shiny shopping bags with fancy labels. I could see tissue paper sticking out of both of them. It took a moment before I regained control of my voice.

"What's that?"

"Lingerie. For you."

Did I laugh? Did I think he was joking? Or did I realize at once that he was totally serious? In any case, it took a few seconds before I murmured that I wasn't accustomed to such things. Meaning, to receiving gifts. I wasn't used to this sort of situation at all.

Alex finally took off his sunglasses and looked right at me.

"Let me do this. Let me take care of you."

There they were again. Those words that caressed my skin and left a warm feeling in their wake. *Take care of you.* Something opened inside of me. I imagined allowing myself to be cared for, lowering the walls. Not having to rely solely on myself. Letting someone past my meticulously polished façade. Was that really possible? Did I dare?

"How do you know what size I wear?"

My voice was barely more than a whisper. Alex looked me in the eye, his gaze unwavering.

"Because I see you. I mean, I really see you. I truly do. And I want you to know that."

It wasn't merely what he said, but *how* he said it. With emphasis. It silenced me. I couldn't utter a single word. I just sat there and stared at him while he stared back. It felt like he could see into me, into the depths of my soul. As if, somehow, this stranger understood who I was and what I'd been through. I took a deep breath, and my body moved of its own accord. My hand went around Alex's neck, my lips pressed against his. He went up to my apartment with me, and we drew all the curtains. There, in the shadows, our story began. And in the shadows it would continue.

I'm shivering. The sun can't penetrate the thick foliage. The light here on the island isn't warm and golden like up at the cabin. Instead, it's a hazy gray. One leg has fallen asleep, and I shift position, placing my feet back on the muddy ground.

Through the soles of my shoes, I feel some sort of current. At first, I ascribe it to the increased blood flow in my legs. But then I make a slight movement, and a powerful whirl of energy rises up from the earth, circles my ankles and calves, takes hold of me. I shout and jump up, yanking my feet away. A hissing sound issues from somewhere, followed by a long, drawn-out smacking sound when the mud lets go of me.

I set off, heading as far away from the middle of the island as I can go, trying to take deep breaths to calm down. But it's not easy. My body is shivering in spite of the heat. To be pulled down into the dunes. Could that happen here? Has it already happened? Are Alex and Smilla—helpless, their screams muffled—somewhere beneath my feet? Fragments of the horror stories about Lake Malice that Alex told echo again through my mind. *No!* I do my best to push aside the ghastly scenes that are creeping into my consciousness. *No, no, no.*

All of a sudden, I'm at the water's edge. This side of the island is rimmed with rocks, both big and small. Some are sticking up from the surface, others lurking underwater, covered with swaying algae. It looks both enticing and dangerous. I squint to look across the lake, measuring with my eyes how far it might be from here to the mainland. Too far, I quickly conclude. Smilla can't swim. She hasn't yet learned how to swim. But she does love to play in the water, like a reckless little daredevil.

I look back down at the silent rocks. Did Smilla decide to go wading and venture too far out? Did Alex take off his shoes and wade in after her, but slip and hit his head on a rock? I close my eyes to ward off such disastrous thoughts. But they only get worse.

Did some force—the same force I seemed to encounter last night when I stared over the side of the boat into the lake as I waited for Alex and Smilla to come back—lure them out into the water, blinding them and leading them straight into a death by drowning? I gasp. I slap my face to drive out all such terrible thoughts. But this time it takes quite a while before my pulse slows and my shoulders sink back into place.

Now that I've searched nearly the whole island, I'm more convinced than ever that they're no longer here.

Slowly, I start walking along the shoreline. I shouldn't let myself get so upset. The mud grabbing my foot was just my imagination, another phantom in my jittery mind. The lake does not possess evil forces. Nor does the island. The idea that two people—a grown man and a four-year-old girl—could be sucked down into the dunes or drawn into the water by evil forces is the stuff of movies and books. And lousy ones, at that. So why do I feel so anxious?

I realize why. I stop next to an area that looks like a campsite, and the answer comes to me. If nothing supernatural is going on, there has to be some rational explanation for Alex and Smilla's disappearance. And that is far more frightening.

I stare at the ground. Between a green tarp and a dirty old mattress, I see a pile of charred wood. Scattered around this primitive fire pit are cigarette butts and empty beer cans. And a knife. A knife with a stained blade. I move closer, bend down, and carefully study the area around the mattress. I don't really know what I'm looking for. Something that could lead me to Alex and Smilla. On one side of the mattress, I see a shriveled condom. Memories of what Alex did to me the other night flood over me. I flinch and step back, disgusted.

My foot lands on something squishy, and I look down, expecting more mud. Instead, I find myself staring straight into a pair of glassy eyes the size of peppercorns. Tiny legs stick out from under my shoe. I jerk my foot away but can't stop staring at the brownish-red jumble of intestines and guts lying on the ground. When I finally realize what I'm looking at, the merciless nausea returns. It's a squirrel. A disemboweled squirrel. I spin around and vomit into a juniper bush. Then I flee.

8

In the middle of the lake, I reduce speed and finally cut the motor completely. I take off my shoes and lean over the side of the boat to rinse them. I tell myself that another animal could have attacked that squirrel. Maybe a fox or a cat. I don't want to think about the knife lying nearby or what it might have been used for. I throw up again, this time into the lake. The vomit claws at my throat. I wipe my mouth with the back of my hand and then have to rinse that off too.

With an effort, I force myself to focus on what I should do next. My search was fruitless, but I can't give up. I refuse to give up. Again, I picture Smilla's smiling face, her dimples and chubby cheeks. Feeling a pang in my heart, I straighten my spine to summon more strength. Then I survey the area around me. Lake Malice is big, much too big for me to take in its whole expanse from this position. But what I do see can only be described as a summer paradise. Glinting sunlight, gentle ripples on the water, numerous docks where skiffs and small motorboats bob at their moorings, and two separate swimming areas, one of them with a diving tower. All around the lake are cottages and cabins of various sizes. Some of them are set so close to the shore that I can see the red-painted gables and flagpoles. Others, like the cabin that belongs to Alex's family, are clustered farther from the water.

I twist around to look first in one direction, then the other. I let my gaze sweep along the shore, moving from house to house. No sign of life anywhere. The summer's over, and Marhem's sun-worshippers are gone. For most people, fall means a return to daily routines, to school and their jobs. That's one of the reasons why we came now. For some peace and quiet. To be alone.

The breeze picks up, spraying cold drops onto my arms. I shiver, noticing the clenching in my stomach. Something is moving in there, something that is me, and yet is not me. Maybe it's not just the summer that's over. Maybe life as I know it is coming to an end. How can I go on? Will I be able to handle all this? Or will it defeat me?

Suddenly, I'm sitting very close to the side of the boat, leaning over and staring into the dark water. Something is drawing me down, down. I can't look away, can't even blink. Then I hear something. It gets louder, rising from a muted humming to a whirring, then to a whispering, a hissing. Like a distant voice, the sound rises up from the water, becoming more frightening, more ominous. I shudder, realizing that I should get out of here. I should clap my hands over my ears and close my eyes. But I seem to have lost all ability to blink or to turn away. And my hands are clamped on the gunwale of the boat. Out of the corner of my eye I see my knuckles, hard and white.

Then I lift up, raising my body until I'm no longer sitting down but leaning forward over the side. I am physically doing the moving, but I'm not the one in charge, not the one deciding. Someone—or something—else has taken command of my body. I feel a rocking under my feet. My weight tips the side of the boat, taking me closer to Lake Malice's dark, mysterious eddies. As if the lake is opening for me, wanting to make the decision easier. A slight movement would be enough, a step forward, a leap into the air. That would be sufficient. I would slice through the surface of the water and then continue down into the deep. That's all I would need to do. Nothing more, never anything more. I would simply fall. Fall freely, out of time, through eternity. Like Papa. Exactly like Papa.

9

The last night. The night Papa disappeared, when he fell out of our lives. Considering how much it affected me, you'd think the images that play in my mind would be detailed and clear. Razor sharp. But they're not. The more crucial the detail from that night, the closer I get to the truth about what happened, the more impenetrable the fog becomes surrounding the events.

What I do remember is what happened before, the little things. For instance, there was a change in the weather a couple of days earlier, and it got colder. From where I was hiding in the dark outside Mama and Papa's bedroom, I could feel a cool breeze seeping into the apartment. The parts of my body not covered by my nightgown, my calves and feet, quickly grew cold. The fresh air was mixed with the smell of smoke. I didn't need to peek into the room to know what that meant. Papa had opened the tall bay window and was perched on the windowsill with a cigarette hanging from his lips. And he was probably holding a drink in his hand. I could tell by the way his voice sounded. It was loud and scornful. Mama's was low and bitter. They were repeating the usual accusations, the same old complaints.

Why do you have to . . . ?
Don't you understand how humiliating it is for me when . . . ?
Cunt.

I clutched my old teddy bear under my arm. A couple of months earlier, I had turned eight. I was a big girl now. That's what all the grown-ups said. But I still slept with Mulle every night. I hugged his body, once so woolly but now matted and worn, as I lay in bed and dreamed of a time that must have existed, though I could no longer really remember. A time when Mama and Papa were happy together. A time before Papa began coming home late at night with strange smells on his skin and clothes. Before I could hear Mama crying through the thin walls of the apartment and Papa swearing loudly in reply.

A cunt. That's what you are.

I flinched and pressed Mulle against my face, squeezing my eyes shut. There it was again. The word Papa used whenever he ran out of arguments. *Cunt.* For some reason, that particular word got under Mama's skin, deflated her, demolished her. But Papa kept right on hurling it whenever they argued. Even though he knew how much it hurt her. Or maybe because of it.

The choice of swear words wasn't the only thing that was repeated. My parents' fights also followed the same pattern, based on the same building blocks. When that particular curse was uttered, it meant the end was near. And a resounding silence would soon set in. At first, Mama and Papa's argument on that particular night seemed to unfold predictably. There was nothing to indicate that this argument would be the fateful exception to the rule. Mama had gone on the attack, this time because of a stain on his shirt collar, and Papa had responded with a scornful remark. She demanded an explanation and an apology, but he refused. When she pressed him, he pulled out his sharpest weapon. And once again, the air rushed out of Mama.

It was right then, after I'd already turned around to tiptoe back to my own room, that the fight rapidly and unexpectedly changed character. They kept going, even though it should have been all over. Their voices sounded distorted and hateful in a whole new way.

I know what you did to Greta. Hitting your own child . . . How could you?

The words reverberated like gunshots. Then it was quiet in there. I froze. There was a rushing in my ears, and I saw it again: the raised hand whistling through the air and slapping me across the face. An image, an event, I'd pushed out of my mind. Now it came back, overwhelming me, striking me full force.

I let go of Mulle, dropping him on the floor. My hand flew up of its own accord and pressed protectively to my cheek. But it was too late. The sting of the slap had already set in. It felt like a thousand sharp and burning-hot needles pricking my skin. *Greta, sweetie, I didn't mean to do it. I just turned around and saw . . . You know I didn't mean to, right? I think it would be best if we don't tell anyone about this.*

And I knew at once who *anyone* was. There was no need to say it out loud. There was only one person from whom it was important to hide what happened. My eyes filled with tears of shock and humiliation as I promised to keep quiet, knowing it was for the best. But now. Now that *anyone* had found out.

I know that I turned around, and, instead of going back to my room or continuing to hide in the shadows, I stepped into the light and stood in the doorway to Mama and Papa's bedroom. I know that it took a moment before they noticed me, and before that happened, the silence ended and their voices started up again. I think I heard questions about how and who and why hurled around, but it's at this point my memory starts to resist. What happened next, the commotion that must have ensued . . . escapes me. Yes. That's exactly how I usually describe it.

Of course that wasn't what I said at the time, right afterward. When curious friends and their equally inquisitive but more discreet parents asked me what happened, I told them nothing. Not a single word. Because I had no words. None were adequate. It was only much later, as the years passed and I grew up, that I began to understand that what happened would never sink into oblivion. Even though Mama and I moved, changed jobs, changed schools, people kept asking and wondering and staring in horror. Finally, I came up with a phrase, one sentence that silences or at least deflects further interest. I have no close friends, but I use the phrase with coworkers and in social settings. I've used it on the psychologists I've seen, and when I told the story to Alex.

It escapes me.

An excellent turn of phrase, if I do say so myself.

10

When I get back to the dock, the sun has slipped behind the clouds. I tie up the boat as best I can. While I'm fumbling with the mooring line, I picture Alex's hands, so dexterous they are as they loop and knot. Something gleams between his fingers. A black silk tie. I jump up, trembling, and wrap my thin cardigan tighter around me. My hand flutters automatically to my throat, and I take several deep breaths.

Instead of taking the narrow path up to the cabin, I choose to detour along the gravel road that snakes around the lake. I need to widen my search area. On one side, I pass several red-painted cabins. I walk up to the houses and shout hello, but no one answers. The windows and doors are closed, the rooms visible behind the lace curtains dark and empty. Yet I can still see patio furniture and flowerpots outside. On the weekend, these cabins will once again be filled with lively activity. Cars will pull into the yards, and doors will open. Tired but happy grown-ups will carry in suitcases while eager children run around, restless after sitting still for so long. Bright voices and infectious laughter will echo between the buildings. But right now it's quiet and desolate. Or is it?

Like a trespasser, I sneak even closer. I can't stop myself. I peer through the dirty windowpanes, try the door handle on an outbuilding. But nowhere do I see any sign that Alex and Smilla have been here, much less that they're here now. Of course not. I continue along the road, pausing now and then at a cabin that is more isolated or looks especially dilapidated. My imagination runs wild. I picture Alex and Smilla, bound and gagged in some cramped and windowless space. My shouts grow more frantic, my footsteps more rushed. Once again, I'm struck by a feeling of phoniness, like there's something fake and affected about my thoughts and actions. As if my search is nothing but a chimera. As if I do have access to the truth, but I choose not to see it. In front of a timbered cabin with gingerbread trim, a solitary yellow plastic swing hangs from a big willow tree, swaying gently in the wind. Smilla loved to swing. My throat tightens. *Loves.* Not *loved.*

The nausea is back, and I have to slow down. I try to throw up, but nothing comes out. My body feels both listless and agitated. As if my whole being is the object of an internal battle, a tug-of-war between cool logic and irrational emotion. And it's not just because Alex and Smilla have disappeared. The fact is that it's been like this ever since the day I staggered out of the clinic, shaken and dumbstruck, with the doctor's words ringing in my ears. Even though it's impossible to see the lake from here, I automatically turn in that direction. I picture myself out in the boat a short while ago and recall how the thought of joining Papa had briefly occurred to me. To be or not to be, that is the question. And now it demands an answer.

I walk with my eyes on the ground, not wanting to see any more swings hanging from trees or abandoned toys on lawns. Instead, I concentrate on placing one foot in front of the other. My pink sneakers keep moving forward. I left my new sandals with the ankle straps and heels back at the cabin. This hasn't turned out to be the sort of vacation I was expecting. My feet work their way forward, one step at a time. I walk and walk. Past more cabins and gardens, and then, as the gravel road curves, I keep going into the woods.

Papa would have liked my sandals. He appreciated pretty things, had an eye for beauty. Every time I dressed up as a princess—and that was frequently—he would clap his hands and shower me with praise about how lovely I looked. Mama, on the other hand, merely shook her head and pressed her lips together. Papa would sometimes come home and hand me a package containing a glittery tiara, stick-on earrings in garish colors, or even lipstick. Mama would take away the lipstick and remark sharply that there were more important things for little girls to focus on than how they looked.

On those rare occasions when my parents would fight in the daytime, Papa might come find me afterward and ask me to put on one of the tulle dresses he'd given me and then offer to pretend we were going to a royal ball together. Mama never came to find me. Not even once. In the aftermath of a heated argument, she would instead withdraw somewhere to be alone, to the bathroom or bedroom, though what she preferred most was to go out for a long walk.

If I showed her my high-heeled sandals, she would call them impractical and wonder how I could walk in them. Didn't they hurt my feet? That's how Mama is. Her disappointment in me has always been disguised as concern. Even though she's never actually said so, I know that she thinks I could've done much better for myself. Sometimes I think she's ashamed of me and the choices I've made. Her job involves dealing with human relationships and conflicts, people's lives. And that sort of thing has real value. Yet she has a daughter whose professional life is devoted to façades, to outward appearances. A daughter who is following in her father's dubious footsteps. Even—perhaps most importantly—when it comes to her personal life. *Alex.* Thinking about him and Mama in the same breath heightens my discomfort. At the very beginning of our relationship, I'd told Mama about him. I couldn't help it. But of course she displayed no joy; she had no sympathy or understanding to offer me. *How could you, Greta?* was all she said. *How on earth could you?*

A movement by the side of the road pulls me out of my brooding. I stop abruptly, looking at a black shape huddled in the ditch before it slowly rises. Before my eyes, the figure takes on human form. I see arms and legs and long, straggly hair, but no eyes. No face at all. I feel my whole body freeze in terror. My fingers instinctively curl into fists. Then the creature turns and something pale, almost ghostly, becomes visible under the mane of hair. The face of a girl.

11

At this distance she seems no older than ten or twelve. Forcing myself to move forward, I see as I get closer that the girl at the side of the road must be in her early teens. But she has a slender body, as thin as a much younger child's. And she's very pale, even though we're at the end of a long and unusually sunny summer. She's wearing a loose-fitting shirt and long pants. Both garments are black, without any pattern or trim. Her hair hangs down her back, and I can't help thinking that it would have been beautiful if only she hadn't dyed it a lifeless black. She looks anxious and keeps glancing over her shoulder.

I stare at her as if bewitched. I realize that she's the first living creature, other than Tirith, that I've met since Alex and Smilla disappeared. I'm very close to her now, and I'm just about to say hello when I see a group of people a few yards away in the woods, near the shoreline. A couple of them are moving back and forth, looking down at the water and then out across the lake, as if searching for something. The others are facing each other, speaking in low voices. The cloud cover lifts, and the sun appears in the sky. The rays strike the shiny, sharp object one person is holding. A flash of light. I flinch and step back.

I must have made a sound, a gasp, or maybe even a stifled shriek, because at that precise moment they all turn around. Pale, angular faces swivel toward me, five or six pairs of eyes stare in my direction. Teenage boys. That's what I manage to think before, as if on cue, they start coming toward me through the trees. Something inside of me, some basic instinct, tells me to flee, to run away as fast as I can. But my legs feel suddenly heavy and wobbly, and my feet seem glued to the ground. The boys are not in a hurry. They move slowly but deliberately. Finally they reach the gravel road and spread out around me. One of them circles halfway around and stops behind my back.

The last one to reach the road is the boy holding the knife. He moves with obvious self-confidence, ignoring me pointedly. He stops next to the girl.

"You were supposed to keep watch."

His hair is the same dull black as hers, but close cropped, with some sort of shaved pattern on the sides.

"Sorry."

The girl leans forward and rests her head on his shoulder in a gesture that looks more submissive than affectionate. He wraps his hand around her head. He moves his other hand across the back of her neck, the whole time keeping a tight grip on the knife. Maybe it was meant to be a tender caress, but it looks like something else entirely.

He turns around and takes a few steps forward so we end up facing each other. He's older than the others. That much is clear. His face is rougher, broader. Instead of a few sparse whiskers around his mouth, he sports a scraggly dark goatee. He has braided the strands and fastened the ends with a row of tiny white rubber bands. But what stands out the most about him are his eyes. It occurs to me that those eyes of his have seen terrible things. And yet he can't be more than twentysomething.

"Who are you? What are you doing here?"

His tone of voice indicates that he's used to being obeyed. I shift my gaze to the girl. She's standing behind him, her shoulders hunched.

Maybe it's his voice, or maybe it's the way she is stooped forward. But something gets into me, making me stand up straight.

"And who are you?"

Without hesitation, he raises his hand, pointing the knife at me. I automatically step back, but bump into a gaunt, hard body. I turn and see cold, narrowed eyes. I turn my head the other way and find a jutting chin and lips pulled into a scornful sneer. My gaze flits away. Downy chins and bright-red zits. T-shirts with stretched-out necklines, worn jeans with rips in the knees. *Kids,* I think. *They're just kids.* Bored kids in a place where nothing much ever happens. They're just trying to scare me. That's all. But I'm not really convinced. Nor does the thought calm me down.

"What are you so fucking scared of? I just need a little manicure."

The young man with the goatee has lowered the knife and is using the point to clean the dirt from under his fingernails. He's rewarded with scattered jeers from the boys standing around me. Then his expression changes again.

"Let's try one more time. Who are you, and what are you doing here?"

He raises his head to look at me. His dark eyes are now impassive. As if he's not seeing another human being in front of him. As if I'm an inanimate object.

"I asked you a question. So answer me."

A sharp jab to my shoulder makes me stagger. The boys move closer. Suddenly, I hear my mother's voice in my head. *Dehumanization,* she says in that annoying professional tone of hers. *There's a profound connection between dehumanization and violent crime.* It's easier to harm someone when you don't perceive them as human, when you can't empathize with the person. So I decide that the opposite argument must also hold true.

I start telling them who I am. I explain that I'm here on vacation. But I don't stop there. I also describe the approximate location of the cabin. And I tell them about Alex and Smilla, that the three of us came here together. I say that they're waiting for me now. That they're going to be worried if I'm not back soon. Then the words stick in my throat and I stop talking. And wait.

Goatee Guy doesn't look concerned. He scratches his arm and glances at his watch. Has he even heard a word I said?

"You haven't taken something that belongs to us, have you?"

At first I think I must have misheard him. *What does he mean?* I frown and shake my head. Hoping, believing, that he'll see I'm genuinely puzzled. Goatee Guy gives me a long look. Then he takes a step closer.

"Are you sure?"

Before I have time to answer, the girl slips next to him, stands on tiptoe, and whispers something in his ear. He listens impatiently, then pushes her away. Out of the corner of my eye, I notice how the other boys are rocking back and forth, casting inquiring glances at Goatee Guy. *What's going on?* The seconds fly by. The only sound is birds chirping. My mouth is dry, and my body is tensed like a taut bowstring.

At last, Goatee Guy makes a nearly imperceptible motion with his hand and turns his back on me. He moves a short distance away. Time stops for a few moments. Then, slowly, I feel the iron ring surrounding me begin to loosen. I'd like to think there's a certain relief in the boys' retreat. But maybe it's mostly disappointment that emanates from their frustrated bodies. Disappointment at having to release their captive. Apparently Goatee Guy notices it too and understands the group's need for one last show of force. I've hardly relaxed my tensed shoulders when he spins around and strides over to me again. In one swift movement, he raises the knife and places the tip under my chin. He doesn't press hard, but the blade is sharp, and terror sinks its claws into me.

"If I find out you're lying . . ."

He doesn't finish the sentence. Instead, he shoves me backward after one last meaningful look. Then he turns around, crosses the ditch, and heads for the shore without looking back. His underlings grin and take a few harmless swipes at me before they follow. I hear their laughter echoing off the trees and see them giving each other high fives. The girl and I are alone on the gravel road. Our eyes meet. Then I turn around and leave.

I walk as fast as I can without actually running. Only after I've rounded the next curve in the forest road and put some distance between me and the kids do I become aware that my heart is pounding fast, that I'm shaking all over. I collapse on the side of the road. I curl up in a ball, making myself as small as possible, all the while keeping an eye on the direction I've just come from. I want to be ready in case they change their minds. Not that it'll really make any difference. If they decide to come after me, I have no way of defending myself.

Squatting there on the ground, I lower my head and once again fix my eyes on my shoes. My pink sneakers. I think of the black shoe I found on the island. The girl by the ditch had a similar pair. A shapeless fear strikes me in the solar plexus, propelling me to my feet. Again I set off down the road, looking over my shoulder every few seconds. I keep expecting to see them racing toward me with their baggy and faded T-shirts flapping around their skinny bodies. But no one is following me. Even so, I run as fast as I can, until my throat is burning and my lungs wheeze. I have to get out of here. Right now.

12

I don't understand where it's coming from, all this hatred inside me. How can my heart have room for so much darkness? Especially someone like me, who was conceived and carried and raised with love. Carefully, she held me in her hands, showing me the path into life. She was at my side, giving me everything, living solely for my sake.

And many years later, when it was my turn to receive the miracle of life, I did the same. Ten tiny toes, ten tiny fingers. Everything changed, and I bowed my head, asking for mercy. I sacrificed everything, not because I was forced to do so, but because I wanted to. I did it gladly. I did it out of love.

I lean forward and bathe her forehead. Even though beads of sweat have formed, her skin is very cold. I want nothing more than for her to sit up and talk to me. Assuage my pain with her love. The space that is mine is so small, and yet I'm not allowed to be left in peace. There, sprouting in the cracks of what once existed, is hatred. Somewhere far away, a voice is speaking. It says: Without me, you are nothing.

I reach for her hand, clasp it in my own. Her fingers are limp. I'm the one who has to keep us together now.

I think how the only thing of importance is that she recovers, that she comes back to me. If only I'm allowed to keep her, nothing else matters. Then I shake off what I know and move on. I can forget. I can even forgive.

That's what I'm thinking, but it's not true. Because whatever happens, I will never be able to forgive you. Do you hear me? Never.

13

The road divides, giving me the opportunity to loop back in the direction of the cabin without having to pass the spot where I met those kids. Somehow I manage to make my way home. By the time I get there, my hips and legs feel like jelly. The marks in the gravel on the road are no longer clear, as if someone has swept them away while I was gone. *The one who stayed and the one who left.*

I limp toward the front steps and root around until I find the key underneath. In the entryway, I'm confronted by my own face in the mirror on the wall. My eyes are like two big patches of soot, and garish pink blush shimmers on my cheekbones. But underneath the plastered-on layers of color and shadow I'm totally pale. I picture the knife in front of me, see the flash of the sharp blade as the young man cleans his fingernails. I feel the point pressing against the delicate skin under my chin.

I stand there in the hall for a long time. The fear slowly ebbs away, but the images refuse to leave me. In spite of what I went through, there's one image that lingers in my mind. It's the image of the long-haired girl leaning against Goatee Guy's shoulder with such trust, such compliance. And the way he responded by sweeping the knife in an arc over the back of her neck. I can't tear myself away from the mirror, and my face suddenly seems to merge with the girl's features there in the glass. Wasn't there something special about her gaze? Didn't I see something gleam in her eyes when she noticed the mark on my throat? Something naked, something familiar. I hear myself talking, see the girl watching me. *My husband and my daughter,* I said, *they're at the cabin waiting for me.* Did she see through me? Did she realize I was lying? I picture her standing on tiptoe, cupping her hand around Goatee Guy's ear. What was it she whispered to him?

I turn away, lean my back against the wall, and slide down to the floor. The minutes pass as the tension slowly seeps out of my body. I have no energy to get up. It feels like I'll never be able to move again. My limbs sag, go slack. Just as my head sinks to my chest, a sharp noise slices through the silence and jolts me awake. My cell phone is in the pocket of my capris. I can feel it vibrating against my thigh. It must be Alex. *It's all over now. Thank God, it's over.* I shove my hand in my pocket, pull out the phone, and raise it to my ear without checking the number on the display.

"Greta?"

Mama again. My head falls back, thudding against the wall behind me.

"Hello? Greta . . . are you there? Is everything okay?"

I mutter something unintelligible in reply.

"What'd you say? I can hardly hear you, Greta. Where are you? I know you're not home because I phoned several times, and you didn't . . ."

I think to myself that I can't stay here in the cabin even one more minute. I need to get in the car and drive away from here. Go to the police. *Or home. You could drive home.*

"I can't talk right now," I manage to say. My voice is somewhere between a wheeze and a whisper. "I have to go."

But Mama is not to be put off so easily.

"What's going on with you, Greta? You're behaving so strangely. These last few days . . . I don't know what you're up to, but I have to say that . . ."

Whatever she was on the verge of saying, whatever was so important, fades to silence. The thought crosses my mind that maybe for once it will be my mother who ends our conversation in a fit of anger. Maybe she's finally had enough. But I hear her take a deep breath, preparing to say something more.

"It's no wonder Katinka's worried about you."

Katinka? Worried about me? I feel hot and cold at the same time. *What did Katinka say? And why has Mama been talking to her?*

"I was at the mall today and dropped by the shop to say hello. But you weren't there. They told me you were on vacation. I had no idea you were planning to take time off right now."

"Mama, I . . ."

"So I ran into Katinka in the shop. As I understand it, the two of you are close friends."

Mama falls silent. All I can hear is her breathing. Is she waiting for me to say something? To offer some comment about my relationship with Katinka? Or is she thinking about the best friend she once had?

I used to eavesdrop on their phone calls, all those long heart-to-hearts. Of course, Ruth was the one who did most of the talking. Mama would mostly sit in silence, hunched over in bed or at the kitchen table.

No, he's not here, as usual. Who knows where he is tonight?

Then she would listen intently, in a way she never did with anyone else. Sometimes she was silent for so long that, if I held my breath, I could hear Ruth's voice on the phone. I couldn't make out what she was saying, but I understood that, whatever it was, Mama considered her words wise and consoling. She would always say something like: "What would I do without you, Ruth? Thanks for listening. I have no one else to turn to."

As I understand it, the two of you are close friends.

Is there something ominous, even menacing, in Mama's words? After what happened, did she lose faith, not only in Ruth but in female friendships in general? Is she afraid Katinka will betray me the same way that Ruth betrayed her? There's nothing to worry about on that score. That's what I'd tell her if she asked. I know better than Mama did. I know better than to confide everything, reveal everything. Katinka may think we know each other well, but that doesn't mean we're close, at least not in the sense Mama and Ruth once were. Definitely not. I did learn something from Mama's mistakes, after all. I hear her clear her throat.

"At any rate. According to Katinka, you haven't seemed quite right lately. Apparently you've called in sick a lot, and . . . well . . . That's actually how she phrased it: that she's worried about you."

I raise my hand to rub my forehead. Again I'm thinking about what happened in the woods. Those kids, the knife pressed to my throat. *What about you?* I want to ask. *Are you worried, Mama? You should be.* But when I open my mouth, something totally different slips out.

"I'm pregnant."

I don't know why I tell her. Maybe to shock her. Or maybe because I'm not myself at the moment. To be honest, I haven't been myself for a long time. Katinka's right. I hear my mother gasp.

"Pregnant? My God!"

She sounds horrified. Then I can hear her pulling herself together. Her voice takes on a new tone. A certain harshness.

"Who's the father?"

I can't do this anymore. I simply can't. I hang up and stumble into the bedroom. I turn off my phone before plugging it in, then fling myself across the double bed. Apathy spreads through me, blocking out all feeling. Just before my eyes fall shut, I see my mother's expression of displeasure. *How could you, Greta? How on earth could you?*

14

Alex's voice wakes me. *It's all in your head.* That's what I think I hear him whisper. *Surely you don't think this is real? You're just imagining everything.* The duvet underneath me is crumpled and damp, and I shiver. Then I feel something next to my leg, something warm, and when I look down I see Tirith curled up against me. I reach down to slip my hand under his soft belly and pull him up to my chest. I slide my finger under his pink collar and scratch the back of his neck. He yawns, giving me a long look through narrowed, sleepy eyes. Smilla's cat. Maybe he's thinking the same thing I'm thinking: *The two of us don't really belong together.* Yet here we are, left to our own devices.

Barely conscious of what I'm doing, I raise my other hand to my throat, touching the dark patch there. Then my fingers move up to my chin. The feeling of that knife is still fresh in my mind. I picture the young man with the goatee. I see his indifferent expression and hear his threats. Hurriedly, I dismiss the image and return my attention to Tirith. I stroke and caress his fur until he luxuriously stretches his black-and-white body across my chest. He meows, a long, drawn-out sound. *Guess we'll just have to stick together,* I imagine him saying. But for some reason, it offers me no consolation. For some reason, it makes me uneasy.

I push the cat away and sit up, a little too quickly, grimacing when I feel the burning inside my throat. Yet another symptom, according to the doctor. Nine weeks along, she told me. Since then, another two weeks have passed, and the change in my body is already noticeable. Nausea and vomiting. Lack of appetite. Aching in my hips. And fatigue. A weariness that seems to have totally taken over. Hesitantly, I place my hand on my stomach, on top of the growing bulge. And then I try out the thought again, the one that has occurred to me many times since I sat in the clinic and heard the news. But no, I've made up my mind. *To be or not to be, that is the question.* This time, the course is set. I want this baby. In spite of everything.

Who's the father? The memory of my mother's words pierces like a sharp blade through my bleary consciousness. Suddenly, I'm wide awake. I turn on my phone and see that I've received three new voice-mail messages. My pulse quickens, but of course, they're all from my mother.

"I'm so sorry, sweetie. I was just so shocked, and . . . We'll solve this somehow. Call me back and let's talk!"

"Or should I come over? Just tell me where you are."

"Please, Greta. Don't do this. I just can't . . ."

Mama's voice breaks. Is she crying? For my sake? I listen to her last message again, and the door that was about to open slams shut. *I just can't.*

The phone slides across the floor when I push it away. Once again, it's all about my mother's needs and how she feels, what she can or can't do. Just like back then, after Papa. Just like it's always been.

I get up, then pause for a moment, staring at my phone. I should really leave it lying there on the floor. Alex isn't going to call.

I gather up the essentials and slip my purse over my shoulder. Then I kneel down, retrieve my phone, and slip it into my purse. My eyes are automatically drawn to the smaller bedroom as I pass, and my feet carry me inside. I sink down on the edge of the bed and clumsily stroke the duvet cover, printed with a fairy-tale princess. Smilla loves princesses. Just like I did when I was her age. We're alike in so many ways. With dry eyes, I press my face against the pillow, breathing in the fading scent of baby shampoo.

"I never got a chance to tell you the good news," I murmur. "You're going to have a little sister or brother."

Far down, deep inside my stomach, I sense a gurgling movement. The fetus moving? No, that can't be. Not yet. Or? Suddenly, I'm seized with shame. An adult who fails, who gives up. Is that the sort of role model I am? The mother that I'm on my way to becoming? No, I have to believe it will turn out fine. Everything that has happened and what I've decided. I get up from the bed and leave Smilla's room.

As I'm passing the hall mirror, I stop and stare at the image confronting me. My mascara is smeared, my eye shadow blotchy, and my hair is standing on end. I look like a madwoman. Quickly, I repair my makeup and comb my hair. Then I dash out the door and down the steps.

The car starts on the second try, and all I can think about is getting away from here. There's nothing keeping me in Marhem anymore. Only fear and confusion remain. With every passing hour, I'm getting more and more ensnared in something I don't understand, something that's becoming scarier. With a little distance, I'll be able to see better what happened and understand everything that now escapes me, everything that is evading and eluding me.

The car rolls along the narrow gravel road, past other summer cabins very similar to the one I've just left. They're on both sides of the road, looking empty and lifeless. Not a single car is parked outside. Not a soul in sight. There's something unnatural about this absence of life, an entire vacation area deserted and abandoned. The whole place seems unreal. A dizzy sense of being trapped in limbo comes over me.

In spite of the desolation, I suddenly feel that I'm being watched. I glance in the rearview mirror, worried I'll see a bunch of kids in ragged clothes looming behind the car. But there's no one there. And when I think about the girl in the ditch, the young man with the knife and his minions, they no longer seem real. Their shapes fade away, dissolving into thin air. Like phantoms. Did I even meet them? Was it real?

My hands grip the steering wheel harder, and I step on the gas. What's happening to me? Am I losing my ability to separate dream from reality? Madness from reason? Somehow I have to find a way to confirm that what I'm experiencing is real, that I'm not just imagining things or about to go . . . I dismiss that thought from my mind. Grit my teeth and keep driving. I catch a glimpse of something above the treetops in the distance. What is it? Smoke. I can clearly see wisps of smoke rising into the sky. That can only mean one thing.

I've now reached the crossroads. The road on the left leads to the entrance to the highway. The road on the right continues on past more cabins and yards to another part of Marhem. To the area where the smoke is coming from. My foot presses down on the clutch. My hand is resting on the gearshift. I signal to turn left. And then turn right.

15

Slowly, I drive along the winding road that takes me deeper into Marhem and farther from the highway. The thin coil of smoke against the sky is my guiding star. Wherever it's coming from, there are bound to be people. Real people. The kind I can see with my own eyes, who will talk to me and convince me that what I'm seeing actually does exist. That what's going on is real.

In this part of Marhem, the cabins are larger. Most of them are more like houses than cabins, and there's more space between the yards. But here too, everything looks closed up and deserted. I drive at a crawl, letting my eyes sweep from one side of the road to the other, looking for fire. For any sign of other people. Even so, the sound is so unexpected that I flinch. I slow down, listen. A series of muted, fitful sounds. When I realize what I'm hearing, I pull over. My heart is hammering excitedly. A dog barking. That must mean I'm close.

I get out of the car and proceed on foot. On the right side of the road, I see dark trees and flashes of sunlight glinting off a big picture window. The yard is huge but a lot of it is hidden behind a tall fence surrounding the property. As I approach, I crane my neck to peer at the house. It's several stories tall and painted brown, an unusual color around here. I catch a glimpse of glorious flowerbeds and a neatly mown lawn. On the highly polished deck, a charcoal grill is smoldering.

My ears are on high alert, but the only thing I hear now is the rustling of the trees and several birds screeching down by the water. Otherwise everything is quiet.

At that second the barking starts up again, and a black streak comes racing around the corner of the house. It's a big dog with a shiny coat, his tongue hanging out. He's batting a yellow ball with his paws, chasing after it, then stumbling over it. The dog seems so immersed in his game that he's not aware of me standing there, hesitating just outside the fence. Or maybe he's too well trained to bother with strangers.

Out of the corner of my eye, I see something move, making me look up. My gaze is automatically drawn to the top floor of the house. Inside a partially open window, a thin curtain billows. Is someone there? I stand still, not sure what to do. I should stop here, try to make contact. Isn't that why I came? But the thought of having to talk to another person makes me uneasy. *What if they can tell by looking at me?*

I whip around and begin heading back to the car.

"Hello there! Can I help you?"

I spin around and almost fall over, I'm so stunned by the voice. Behind me, an elderly man is standing at an open gate. In spite of the heat, he's wearing pressed trousers and a sweater over his shirt. His hair is thinning, and his expression is friendly, though a bit wary. At his side, standing very close, is the dog. The man has a tight hold on the dog's collar.

"Did I scare you? I didn't mean to."

I shake my head, murmuring something about being fine. But my heart is beating fast, and I have a hard time getting the words out.

"I apologize for sneaking up on you. I have to admit that I'm extracareful right now. There aren't many people left in Marhem this late in the season, and you never know what those kids might get up to. You have to be on guard, that's all there is to it."

I stare at him. *Those kids. So they really do exist. I'm not going . . .* I shake my head, putting on an expression the man seems to take for agreement. He relaxes and smiles, apparently having decided that I'm no threat.

"It's certainly not pleasant," he goes on. "Some nights, they make a huge racket. Down by the water, sometimes out on the island. I try to keep my distance as best I can."

Out on the island? I think about Alex and Smilla. About the black shoe I found when I was searching for them. I shiver. The man introduces himself, but a second later I've already forgotten his name.

"Do you live around here?"

I manage to nod and muster what might pass for a smile.

"In one of the cabins above the dock over that way," I tell him, giving a vague wave of my hand.

"Alexander," he says at once, startling me. "Are you with Alexander? It's been a long time since I last saw him, but I thought I caught sight of him the other day, along with a little girl. I assume she's your daughter?"

"Smilla?" I whisper.

There's something wrong with my voice. It sounds hoarse and raspy. Hollow. But the man doesn't seem to notice. He pats the black dog, who has stuck his wet nose in his hand.

"Smilla. What a lovely name. So you're her mother, Alexander's wife. Actually, I think we've met before. But it was only very briefly."

I lower my eyes. Am I nodding again? Yes, I think I am. But my thoughts are elsewhere. This man says he's seen Smilla. With Alex. *The other day.* What exactly does that mean? In spite of the heat, goose bumps rise on my bare legs.

"When did you say you saw them? Do you remember? Smilla and Alex, I mean. And where exactly did you see them?"

The man frowns. His eyes have gone hazy.

"I think it was near the dance floor, on Midsummer Eve. But that's a few years back now. I seem to remember that you were newlyweds. Those were the days. That's when there was still an active association here in Marhem that organized events."

I stare at him and try again.

"I mean recently. You said you saw them the other day. Where was that?"

The man slowly shakes his head.

"I'm sorry," he says uncertainly. "I don't really remember."

I find myself wondering why he would lie. But then I realize that maybe he's actually telling the truth. He's an old man, and maybe his memory isn't what it used to be. Just because my own relationship to the truth is slippery, it doesn't mean that other people casually toss lies around. The black dog pulls free of his master and comes toward me. He quickly sniffs at me, but when I make an attempt to scratch behind his ears, he retreats. The dog is no longer wagging his tail.

"Well, I'd better be going . . . ," I say, already turning away.

"He looked angry," the man says suddenly. "Alexander, I mean. Or maybe scared. Terrified. Hard to tell which it was."

A gust of wind sweeps past the tree trunks, carrying with it the smell of danger. *Angry. Or terrified. Hard to tell which it was.*

"I'm sorry, but I have to . . ."

I turn around and run. Race away without saying good-bye. Behind me, I can just barely hear the man shout that I should be on my guard, that those kids aren't to be trusted.

The gravel sprays up from the tires when I speed off in the same direction I came from. I hardly notice where I'm driving, aware only that the car is veering from one side to the other. *Angry. Or terrified. Hard to tell which it was.* My stomach is churning and clenching, something is moving restlessly inside. My heart is banging against my ribs. *Little Smilla.*

I don't dare risk it. There's only one thing to do. I know where I have to go.

16

For a long time, I thought of Papa as missing. In the apartment block where we lived, it wasn't uncommon for fathers to leave their families. They would simply pack up their stuff and walk out the door, never to return. That's not what happened with my father. But what difference did it make? He was missing all the same.

Afterward. Seconds afterward. I remember how we stared at each other, my mother and I. How, for a brief moment that seemed like eternity, we shared a wordless connection. We knew. We were the only two people in the world who knew what had just happened. But then she turned her back to me, breaking eye contact. I don't really know what happened after that. Except that we moved apart, that she shut me out. I was a child, but I wasn't stupid. I understood that I was to blame. That it was all my fault. But her rejection still hurt.

Sirens wailing on the street below, blue lights flashing across the front of the building. The front door standing open to the stairwell, men and women in dark uniforms, their faces tense, going in and out of the apartment. Throughout all of it, the door to Mama and Papa's bedroom remained closed. Desperate sobbing—at times, a hysterical scream—issued from inside. I sat on the floor in my room. Clutching Mulle, waiting in silence. I didn't know what else to do. I just knew that if I didn't stay there until the door in front of me opened, until Mama came in and put her arms around me, then I might as well disappear from the earth. Me too.

Two men in dark uniforms tried to talk to me. *The police,* they said. *We're with the police.* At first, they stood there, then they crouched down. They asked me questions, but I pretended not to hear. When they kept on talking, saying my name and repeating the questions, I began humming to myself. If I pretended that everything was the same as usual, maybe it would all go back to normal. Maybe I could make the bad thing that happened disappear. All I had to do was not think about it. Finally, the older policeman took me by the arm and spoke firmly. I hit him in the face. Then he yelled and took Mulle away from me. He said I was too old for such nonsense. His partner turned pale and looked grim. He pulled the other policeman out of the room and whispered something about *just a kid,* and *in shock.*

Then he came back, the younger one. He sat down next to me and talked to me nicely for a long time, explaining that everything was going to be fine, that the police only wanted the best for me, they wanted to help me. That's why they were here. I realized that he wanted me to trust him, and I tried, at least a little. But that didn't make any difference. It was too late for trust. They had taken Mulle away from me, and I would never forgive them for that.

17

The nearest town is only about a fifteen-minute drive from Marhem. There's not much to it. A pedestrian street with a grocery store, a few small shops, a library, and a police station. I almost expect the station to be closed, but when I reach for the handle of the door, it opens. Afterward, I think to myself it would have been better if the door had been locked, if I'd been forced to wait. Maybe then I could have calmed down and reconsidered. Maybe I would have come to my senses and avoided the chaos that followed.

I speak to a woman standing behind a high counter. Her dark hair is pulled back in a tight ponytail. She gets out a notepad with a form to fill in. Without thinking, I rattle off my name and phone number. That's when everything goes haywire. I try to tell her what happened, but I make a mess of it. I can hear how scattered I sound. For a moment, the policewoman's pen hovers over the paper in front of her. Then she slowly puts it down.

"Malice?" she says. "I haven't heard of any lake with that name."

"That's what it's called," I reply. "By the locals."

"So what's its real name?"

I can't answer that, so I simply throw up my hands and look away for a moment. The woman stares at me. Then she asks me for the names of the people I "think are missing." She also wants to know my relationship to them. I babble and explain, the whole time listening to my own words, hearing how the truth and the lies get tangled up.

"So what do you think is the reason for this . . . disappearance? What would be the most plausible explanation? In your opinion, that is."

It could be the words she uses, but it could also be the way she's looking at me that does it. All of a sudden, my whole body goes cold. A heavy, metallic taste rises in my mouth. *It was a mistake to come here.* I take a step back. Then another. And another. The female police officer is watching me. But she doesn't say anything else. Not even when I brusquely turn on my heel, dash for the door, and practically explode out of the station. She lets me go.

On my way back to Marhem, I have a strong feeling that I'm being followed. A green car is driving too close, and I peer nervously in the rearview mirror, trying to make out what the driver looks like. But he or she has pulled down the visor, and the only thing visible is a solitary dark figure. I tap lightly on the brake, challenging the car behind to keep back. In response, the car veers into the passing lane. As it pulls even with me, I turn my head, but the sun glints on the passenger-side window of the other car, and I can't see who's sitting inside. I can't even tell if it's a man or a woman.

Now I feel my car shuddering underneath me, and the steering wheel seems to leap out of my hands. *What is happening?* I'm completely bewildered. I'm on the verge of tears. Then I realize that it's not the car or the steering wheel that's moving. It's my body shaking uncontrollably.

I slow down, pull over, and stop. I don't care that it's probably illegal to park here. With my pulse racing in my throat, I stare at the green car as it disappears around the curve. I hear a muted ringing coming from my purse. *My phone!*

I can tell at once. I can feel it in my whole body. This is an important phone call, one that I shouldn't miss.

I throw myself onto my purse, which I'd tossed on the seat beside me, clawing and rummaging like a woman possessed. The contents spill out onto the passenger seat. A compact, lipstick, and a pair of dangly earrings. My hands are still shaking, but I manage to find my phone and pick it up. Wild eyed, I stare at the display. Unknown number. With trembling fingers, I press the "Answer" button and hold the phone to my ear.

"Yes?"

My voice is barely above a whisper. When the person on the other end starts talking, it takes me a moment to figure out who it is. Because it's not Alex. It's not Smilla. It's not even my mother. It's the police officer.

"Greta," she says authoritatively, "I'm the officer you spoke to at the police station. I have . . . Well, you might say that I've looked into the matter. And I found something strange. Do you know what I'm talking about?"

She falls silent. Neither of us speaks. I reach out my right hand and fumble around the passenger seat until I find something to hold on to. I clutch it tightly. Steeling myself.

"I should have checked on the information you gave me while you were here, but . . . Well, you left rather quickly. But now I've done a search in the records, and what I found—or rather, what I didn't find—surprises me. Let's just say that. And I need your help to resolve the matter."

Through a haze of pain, I hear her again asking me about Alex and Smilla. Were those their names? The people who disappeared? Did we have the same last name, or . . . ?

The police officer doesn't sound unkind, but I can hear in her voice that I don't need to reply. She already knows.

"Is this information correct?"

Now she's rattling off my full name and social security number. All the information I gave her at the station, along with my cell phone number. Almost as if . . . I swallow hard. *As if, deep in my heart, I wanted to be found out.* From somewhere far away, I'm aware of a stinging, burning sensation. It's part of me, and yet not. Outside the window, another car rushes past, the horn blaring with annoyance, but I hardly notice.

"Greta?" she says. "Are you still there? Is all of this information correct?"

The pain increases, becoming more blatant. Something is stabbing my body, ripping through my skin.

"Yes," I tell her. "I'm still here. And it's correct."

The pain sends a shudder through my body, and everything swims before my eyes. I force myself to look down at my clenched fist. Blood is seeping through my fingers and over my knuckles. I open my fist and stare at the earring lying in my palm. At the sharp end of the hook, which is right now embedded deep in my hand.

From a distance, I hear the policewoman saying my name again. I murmur something unintelligible. She takes a deep breath. Both of us are preparing for what will come next. For the words that have to be said.

"According to our records, Greta, you are not married. Nor do you have a child. There is no husband or daughter in your life. And never has been."

18

I might as well tell it like it is. I'm not like other people, not normal or reliable in the way most people are. But at least I have enough self-awareness to realize this. Every once in a while, at various periods in my life, I have sought psychological help. The pattern is always the same. I wait until the last minute, until I'm just about to fall apart and my life is on the verge of shattering. That's when I get help. Each time, a different psychologist. I never go back to the same one as before.

Once a week, sometimes more often, I sit down in a worn-out armchair, in which a faceless horde of unfortunate souls has sat before me, and in which others will sit after I'm gone. The rooms are not the same, but they always look similar. A mildly sympathetic face in the chair across from me, a box of tissues on a table between us. And then we converse. Well, maybe that's not really the right word for it. I'm the one who's expected to say things, of course. To explain and elucidate. Turn myself inside out.

With each new psychologist, I hope that this time things will be different. I hope the person seated across from me will be bolder than the previous ones. Won't just settle for asking questions about what really happened to Papa and then wait for me to reply. But instead will be brave enough to look me in the eye and say it out loud. Say that they understand, and then speak the truth. So I won't have to do it myself. Someone else has to release me. I can't do it on my own. But that's never how it turns out.

This usually goes on for a few weeks, sometimes even a couple of months. By then, we will have reached the painful part—or rather, we'll be going in circles without making any progress.

The psychologist leans forward, patiently asks me the question: *So then what happened?* It escapes me, I insist, and the mildly sympathetic face grows tense. The psychologist retreats, tries another angle, asks other questions: *What do you think about . . . ? What makes you . . . ?* Nothing but questions, never any conclusions. So I pay the bill, say that I'm feeling much better now, and walk out of their office and never go back. They offer no objections. They let me go.

Only one of them has ever tried to keep me there. Literally.

That was years ago, before I met Alex. The psychologist was a blond woman, not much older than me. I'd often thought there was something fragile about her, but when I stood up to announce that after this session I was done, that I wasn't planning to see her anymore, she grabbed my wrist and held on. Gently, and yet with surprising firmness.

"If you leave now, it means you haven't learned a thing about yourself, and you won't be any better prepared to confront either the past or the future. Next time you encounter an overwhelming or surprising situation, the pattern will repeat itself."

She stayed seated in her armchair, and when I looked down, I noticed she was wearing a short-sleeved dress. It was the middle of the summer, and the room was hot. Yet there was something about that dress that caught my attention. I frowned.

"Cardigans and jackets," I said to her. "I've never seen you wear anything with short sleeves before."

She shook her head to show that she wasn't about to be distracted.

"Things are going to get worse for you," she went on. "And you risk being knocked off balance. In the worst-case scenario, that sort of state of mind could have very unfortunate consequences. For you, or for those close to you."

I could have yanked my hand away and stormed out of the room. But I didn't.

"What do you mean?"

"Early in life, you learned to adopt certain strategies in crisis situations. You are repeating those same strategies as an adult, even though they're not effective."

"What is it with you psychologists? Why can't you say things so other people can understand?"

She looked at me impassively.

"Okay. I'll say this as clearly as I can, Greta. What I worry you might 'think up' are the same things you did as a child. When you were in shock, when you encountered . . . adversity."

Heat bubbled up under my skin, filling my eyes.

"Telling lies?"

"Yes. Or worse."

I stare at the blood seeping out between my fingers and down my wrist. My whole hand is throbbing with pain. My palm is sticky on the steering wheel. I can no longer understand my own motives. I can't remember my reasoning from when I dashed into the police station, and I can't form a single sensible thought right now.

It feels like the last shreds of reason are spilling out of me along with the blood from the wound in my hand. Am I about to lose control? Is this how those last seconds feel, right before the big breakdown? The blond psychologist, whose office I was finally able to leave—what would she say if she could see me now? *Didn't I warn you?*

The road to Marhem, back to the cabin. I don't know how I manage it, but somehow I drive the whole way without landing in the ditch or crashing into an oncoming car. I press the gas pedal and the brake, signal, and turn, exactly as if I was an ordinary driver, as if nothing has happened.

When I finally pull in and park in the same spot as before, on the gravel road outside the cabin, there's blood everywhere. Blood smeared on the steering wheel and part of the dashboard, blood on my shirt, and bright patches on my capris. But at least the wound has stopped bleeding. *There is no husband or daughter in your life. And never has been.* I shake my head at myself. I should have known better than to go to the police. Should have realized I had to handle this on my own.

I turn the key in the ignition to switch off the engine. I turn toward the passenger-side window and stare out at the road. The other night, there was another car here, right next to mine. It wasn't properly parked, and the engine was running the whole time. That muffled rumbling was like a bass tone under the agitated voice I heard through the partially open window. Agitated? More like hysterical. Voice? More like a howl, a scream of pain and anger. An icy shiver ripples through my body. Should I be worried? Whoever screamed must have noticed the license plate on my car. And maybe, in spite of their frantic state, they memorized it, that particular combination of letters and digits that would make it possible to identify me.

I reach for my purse on the seat next to me, then gather up and stuff inside everything that had fallen out. The palm of my hand tugs and twinges, and I grimace, picking up the earrings with care. *The one who stayed and the one who left.* Afterward, I didn't ask Alex about that nighttime visit. I thought I could put two and two together, that I understood enough. Now I feel a nagging doubt in my mind. What is it I think I understand? At the moment, I seem unable to follow even the simplest train of thought.

Then I'm once again standing in the entryway, on the green and slightly gritty hall rug. I stand there, without taking off my shoes, just listening. At first, there's only silence. Then I hear a sound from the living room. Hesitant, padding steps. I listen and wait. I know who is approaching. When Tirith comes into view, something inside me relaxes and eases. I sink down on my knees and greedily stretch out my hands toward him. The cat's fur feels soft under my fingertips, and I realize how much I've hungered for that—for touch, for contact—these last twenty-four hours. My whole life.

I stroke Tirith's back and scratch behind his ears as he purrs happily. He licks my fingers and sniffs at the wound on my hand. He seems surprisingly interested. Again and again, he presses his nose gently on the clotted blood. Then he seems to make a decision and starts cleaning the wound very thoroughly, running his rough tongue over the puncture. At first I let him do it, thinking now we're connected for life, this cat and I. The past is behind us, and we know nothing about the future, but at this moment, we are joined, merging together. His saliva and my blood.

Then he turns his narrowed yellow eyes toward me, and I impulsively draw my hand away. Slowly I get to my feet. Tirith. An odd name for a pet. Alex was the one who thought of it. I remember when he explained that Minas Tirith means *Tower of the Guard*. I keep my eyes fixed on the black-and-white cat as I fumble for the door handle behind me. We are staring at each other, Tirith and I. One of us inquisitive, the other tense.

"All right," I say at last, my voice sounding so hoarse that I have to clear my throat before going on. "Time for you to go out for a while. Go on now!"

The cat looks away, swiftly forgetting how abruptly I stopped petting him, and saunters out. I close the door behind him and lock it. When I turn around, I catch sight of one of the hooks positioned low on the wall. The fear that stabs at my chest is so strong that I gasp for breath.

Hanging from the hook is a jean jacket belonging to a four-year-old girl. I collapse onto the floor. Thoughts of the unimaginable descend upon me once again. *That can't be true.*

I rub my eyes and only when I see the black streaks of damp mascara on my skin do I realize that I'm crying. *Smilla. I'm sorry.*

But there is no forgiveness to be had. The feeling that I'm a hypocrite, a cheater, again overwhelms me. What good is all this searching for her? The fault is still mine, pressing heavily on my chest along with the thought of everything I could have done differently. What I should have done. What I shouldn't have done. *If only . . .* Then she might still be here.

Finally, I have to pinch myself hard, on my cheeks and my arms, to stop all this. Why do my thoughts keep going down these paths? As if everything is over, as if it's too late. As if Smilla is . . . Suddenly, the fear and guilt are swept away. In their place, a huge wave of fury washes over me. I hurl my purse at the wardrobe door.

"You bastard!" I wail. "What have you done with her?"

But I'm the only one who hears my words. And it's not clear who they're directed at. Or at least that's not something I'm prepared to say aloud. I haven't yet ventured that far into the shadows.

19

It's over. She's gone. I sat there and held her as the life seeped out of her body. And afterward . . . afterward I was still sitting there. I didn't want to move from her side, didn't want to leave her there, but in the end, I had no choice.

She was my anchor, but when the mooring rope was cut, when the arms were ripped from their safe haven, everything fell apart. Now I'm drifting aimlessly. The solid ground on which my life rested no longer exists. The words that resound in my head are more true than ever. Without me, you are nothing.

As I drift, rocked back and forth on the swells of despair, I often summon up pictures of you.

Sometimes you come so close that I think I can stretch out an ice-cold, dripping-wet hand to touch you. I can feel you trembling.

Swift footsteps and low voices nearby, but I'm only vaguely aware of them. Something else feels much more urgent. Like the fact that the walls around us are about to cave in. I can see it, even though no one else seems to notice or understand. Everything is about to collapse, fall apart. First, her life. Now, mine.

I open my mouth, but the scream refuses to take shape. Not yet. But I know that it's there somewhere, that it's getting closer.

Something new will take over, a new voice, a different self. A clenched fist. A howl of fury.

Your life won't be allowed to stay the same either. You too will be shaken to the core. You too will be obliterated.

20

My body is going somewhere, and I follow along. I walk down the narrow path to the dock. It's as if my feet sense that I'm having trouble keeping things together, as if they've taken control and are carrying me forward whether I like it or not. Rocks and tree roots, blueberry sprigs and ferns. It's all so familiar. How many times have I taken this path? When was the last time I was here? Wasn't it quite recently?

As I approach the lake, the ground gets marshier, and there's moss everywhere. Doesn't it seem like an unusual amount of moss? It covers the rocks, trails over roots, and blankets fallen tree trunks. It seems to be slowly but steadily in the process of swallowing up everything in sight. And there's something about the color, the moss-green hue that's awfully green. Almost shiny. It doesn't look natural. More like it's been manipulated by some computer program. What was it Alex whispered to me in my dream? *Surely you don't think this is real? It's all in your head.*

The nausea is creeping back. Alex. His voice, which is still echoing in my head. His hands, which are still burning on my skin. And the memories, all those memories piling up in a dark corner of my consciousness.

When Alex entered my life, everything happened very fast. The emotions that flared up were so intense that the edges soon turned scorched and sooty. We got close, but it was a different kind of closeness from what I'd imagined on those lonely nights when I sat at my kitchen table or in front of the TV. And it's true that he saw me, but with a different eye from the one I imagined that first time he gave me a ride home. We talked very little. The intimacy we shared was almost exclusively physical. I had nothing to compare it to, so I had to resort to what I'd heard and read. I assumed that's the way it is for most people in the beginning. I assumed that's what it feels like to be in love.

Yet I had a sense that I wanted something more, though I didn't know what that might be, was never able to put it into words. And Alex never asked. He was more interested in showing me what he expected. Like the time I woke up to find him trying to get inside me. Dazed with sleep, I screamed in alarm, but he simply put his hand over my mouth. He looked me deep in the eyes, held me close, and moved his body against mine.

"I see you," he said. "Don't be scared. I'm here, and I see you."

And I knew that was true. I was no longer alone. Not with Alex looking at me. It was as if I came alive under his gaze. He made me real. So I surrendered, allowing him to lead the way. And I complied.

I step down into the boat, feeling it rock under my weight. I manage to keep my balance, compensating for the swaying motion. I close my eyes in an attempt to quell the nausea.

It was the incident at the window that marked, in a painful way, the transition from blind passion to something else. We were in the living room of my apartment, and I was naked. Alex had just undressed me. He was still fully clothed when he turned me around, took a firm grip on my upper arms, and dragged me through the room. At first I thought we were heading for the sofa, but then I realized he was moving me toward the window. The tall, narrow window with no sill or curtains. It was twilight and dark both inside and out, but Alex switched on the ceiling light.

I froze, gave an embarrassed laugh, and whispered that someone might see us. He didn't reply, and when I looked over my shoulder and saw the expression on his face, the laughter died in my throat. I tried to resist, but it was too late. He was considerably stronger than me, and soon he was pressing my naked body against the cold windowpane, fully exposed to the neighbors across the street and to passersby below. Alex grabbed the back of my neck with one hand and my wrists with the other, and I remember standing there with my breasts raised and flattened and my nose twisted painfully to the side, trying to understand why this was happening. Why was he doing this? What was the point? If this was just another one of the games he found so amusing, why was he digging his fingers into my neck so hard?

As I recall, it wasn't a conscious decision on my part to give up, to stop fighting him. I remember only that my body went limp and ceased all attempts to get away. As soon as Alex noticed this, he pulled me backward, shoved me down on the sofa, and pulled down his pants. He didn't look me in the eye. Maybe that's why he didn't notice that I was crying until it was over. I remember he seemed almost surprised by my tears, didn't understand why I was so upset. He said he found it arousing knowing someone might see me. He said someone with a beautiful body like mine shouldn't feel ashamed. He said nothing about wanting to humiliate me or hurt me. But maybe he noticed something in my eyes, a trace of revulsion or doubt. The next day, a delivery boy came to the store bearing the biggest bouquet of long-stemmed red roses I've ever seen. The accompanying card said: *From someone who loves mysteries. Yes, loves. Don't ever leave me.*

The water is calm, the surface smooth. It seems wrong to shatter the silence with the sound of the outboard motor, so I decide to row instead. I make sluggish progress. It feels like the water is resisting me, as if it only reluctantly yields to the oars. Dark waves lap against the side of the boat, hissing and whispering. I lean forward, working so hard that sweat trickles down my back. The cut on my hand stings, but I ignore the pain. That's something I'm good at, after my time with Alex.

Finally, I near the island, planning to pull into the same place as usual. The spot where Alex moored the boat before he and Smilla went off on their adventure. The place where I pulled in when I came back to search for them. How many times is that now? My thoughts whirl; everything blurs together. It feels like so long ago that I was last here, and yet . . . and yet it seems like just recently.

The first things I see are the boats. Two rowboats are bobbing in the water close to the island, but on the opposite side from where I was planning to go ashore. The next instant, I notice the group that has gathered, their bodies sticking up like dark shadows from the tall grass between the trees. I know at once who they are, and I freeze midstroke. My boat glides forward in one last, slow movement, and then comes to a halt in the bewitched waters. I can make out their hoarse voices as they talk, interspersed with a laugh or a cough. And then, suddenly, a shrill scream.

My heart lurches. I should turn the boat around and go home. Get out of here before they see me. But I don't. My arms and hands seem to move of their own volition. Cautiously, I begin rowing toward the island again, hunching over the oars. My pulse quickens with every stroke. The words he said, that man in the big brown house, echo in my mind. *Some nights, they make a huge racket. Down by the water, sometimes out on the island. I try to keep my distance as best I can.* A bright glow tells me that the kids have made a bonfire. I think of the primitive fire pit I discovered when I was searching the island and about the green tarp and the stained mattress. The empty beer cans, the cigarette butts, the used condom. And the eviscerated squirrel.

I'm close now. If any of those kids glance over, they'll see me. I hear another scream. This time, it's louder, more piercing. It's a scream of pain. And panic. It cuts right through me, releasing a flood of images, all of them violent. They pour out, jumbled together, flashing past at furious speed, and I can do nothing to stop them. Images of myself and of Smilla, and of that long-haired girl. Images of hands, alternating between tender and rough. And pictures of objects, relentlessly sharp and treacherously soft. Hands and objects that are used to subdue and to harm.

"Stop!" I cry as loudly as I can. "Please, stop!"

I'm on my feet, standing up in the boat, without knowing how that happened. Someone gives a shout. Several kids pop up from the grass or appear from behind the bushes. Only now do I see how many there are. In the middle looms a figure with his hands on his hips. He doesn't move, and his face is hidden in shadow, but I know he's staring at me. I have his full attention.

"Where is she?"

My voice is so hoarse it doesn't carry properly. The young man with the braided goatee doesn't reply. Maybe he doesn't hear my question. Or else he just doesn't care. Suddenly and unexpectedly, I find myself on the verge of tears.

"Please," I shout again, fighting to keep my voice from breaking. "Don't hurt her."

Goatee Guy turns to one of the kids standing next to him. I hear him speak in a low voice, but I can't make out the words. Whatever he says prompts hoarse and derisive laughter. An arm waves in the air. The next moment, something whizzes past me and lands with a splash in the water behind the boat. A rock. And then another. This time, it strikes the bow.

My eyes shift from one kid to another, taking them all in. Searching for the face of a girl. *I know she's there somewhere. I have to save her!* Soon, more rocks are flying over the boat and raining into the water, and I'm forced to raise my arms to protect myself. I think I see one or more of the dark figures heading toward the two rowboats, and I realize I no longer have any choice. My hands move swiftly, and the motor starts up with a roar. I steer away from the island, heading back across Lake Malice.

"Stay away from here. Otherwise, the same thing will happen to you that happened to . . ."

I don't hear the rest of the threat hurled after me, because just at that moment, something hard and sharp strikes my shoulder blade. A burning pain makes me double over. I speed up, feeling my pulse hammering against my eardrums.

It seems to take an eternity, but finally I make it back to the dock. I tie up the boat and rise up on wobbly legs, only to sink down again. I stare at the rock lying in the bottom of the boat. It's big and sharp edged. If it had hit me in the head . . . If that was their intent . . . A shiver ripples across my skin.

What I should do is hurry back to the cabin, lock the door, and hide.

No one seems to have followed me, but if those kids do come and find me here . . . My misgivings fade into nothingness. I refuse to let fear take hold. *So, is it over?* That's what races through my mind instead. *Is it finally over?*

The next second, another thought intrudes. My hands automatically touch my stomach, protecting the life growing inside. A couple of weeks ago, I left the clinic with the doctor's words ringing in my ears. I remember my exact thought: *This isn't like it was with Smilla. This is something different, something completely new.* Emotions surge inside me. Elation. Guilt. Dread.

I didn't tell Alex. Not until we got to Lake Malice. We were eating dinner, and I said no to wine, then gave him a meaningful look. Alex stared at me for a long time, his face impassive.

"I understand," he said at last and took my hand.

His expression was so tender at that moment, so I thought maybe, just maybe it would work out. Maybe if I didn't—

"Have you made an appointment?"

It was his tone of voice that made me realize at once what he meant. He wasn't talking about an obstetrician appointment. An abortion. He wanted me to get rid of our child. I bowed my head and swallowed the food in my mouth without chewing.

"Not yet, but I will," I told him. "As soon as we get back."

Alex gave me a kiss and quickly changed the subject as he helped himself to more food. After dinner, he gave me his orders, took me into the bedroom, and closed the door behind us.

Later that night, I lay awake, my body hurting too much to sleep. All my nerves and muscles ached. I heard the car rumbling outside and the voice screaming. I heard Alex carry Smilla inside and put her to bed in the room next to ours. Even though I was wide awake, I didn't get up to go to them. And when Alex crept back into bed, I pretended to be asleep. But by then, I'd already made my decision. It was perfectly clear in my mind.

I stroke my throat, cautiously touching the skin. Then I bury my face in my hands and bend forward. After a while, my fingers fall away on their own, and my gaze is drawn over the gunwale. I peer down into the water lapping against the side of the boat. I stare into the lake's impenetrable darkness. Even here, so near shore, it's impossible to see the bottom. Staring into Lake Malice is like being sucked into a black hole, a vortex. I'm whisked through the tunnel until I encounter a circular light at the other end. An opening. And there, in the middle of the light, the contours of a man's face appear. *Alex!* A gasp escapes my lips.

I lean forward, closer to the water, closer to the image. That's when I realize it's not a tunnel, but a well. And from its depths, I'm staring up at Alex, who is looking over the edge. Behind him, I glimpse a shadow: someone is sneaking up on him. Someone whose stealth will soon be channeled into a single swift and violent act. Two hands rise up, the palms hurtling through the air to strike Alex on the shoulder blades.

With no time to turn and meet the eye of his assailant, he plunges over the edge and plummets toward eternity, toward the bottom of the well.

And toward me? No, I'm no longer there. I'm up above now, standing in the same place where Alex was standing. I lean forward, cock my head to one side, and squint down into the well, as if I'm searching for someone who disappeared. Then I study my hands, brushing away a thread from Alex's sweater that got snagged on my skin. And I feel a slight ache in the palms of my hands, at the very spot where they just slammed against hard shoulder blades.

My body feels heavy and wobbly as I flee the boat. It rocks alarmingly under my feet, but then I'm once again standing on the dock. As I go ashore, I keep my eyes fixed straight ahead. Unwavering. I refuse to allow my gaze to shift even for a second toward the seemingly harmless ripples in the water, afraid to risk losing myself again in Lake Malice's seductive darkness. I can't handle any more distorted visions.

As I stumble along the path up to the cabin, I'm filled with foreboding. What were those images my subconscious conjured up? My hands shoving Alex, pushing him into the well. Mere fantasies, of course. Compulsive thoughts. Yet all of it seemed so real. Like repressed memories. I think back to when I stared into the water while Alex and Smilla were playing on the island. I remember feeling as if I'd lost all concept of time. How many minutes had actually passed when I regained my senses? Was it only minutes, or could it have been much longer? And what actually happened during that time?

I hadn't thought about that particular detail before, but now it turns me cold. I spot the cabin up ahead and start running. My body protests. I feel tired and weak and tormented, but I ignore all that and keep running. I run to avoid thinking about the fact that, as soon as I came to in the boat, I knew Alex and Smilla were gone. Without even having to search for them.

When I reach the door, I can taste blood in my mouth. *I already knew. How could I have known?*

21

I wake up from a dream, a dream about a bush. Under the bush a leg is sticking out. A cold, pale leg that belongs to a four-year-old girl. It's a leg that is no longer bubbling with life, a leg that will never again do any jumping. I fumble for something on the night table, find an empty teacup, and throw up into it. This time it's mostly just spit and bile that come out of me. I don't need a bigger container.

My face is wet when I roll over in bed. I've been crying in my sleep. This time I don't bother to stretch out my hand, because I know no one is lying next to me. The numbers on the alarm clock glow faintly. It's the middle of the night. Dark on all sides, dark no matter where I turn.

I wipe my cheeks on a corner of the duvet and run my tongue over my front teeth, noticing the sour taste in my mouth. I lie there for a while, wallowing in self-loathing and disgust. As I stare up at the ceiling, other emotions surface, racing through my body, one after the other. One of them lingers longer than the others. *Alone. I'm so terribly alone. Again. How did that happen?*

I slide my hand down my nightgown, pushing the fabric aside to place my hand on the bare skin of my stomach. A rumbling under my palm startles me, but then I realize it's not the fetus moving. Just ordinary hunger pangs. I can hardly remember the last time I ate, much less wanted to.

I stretch my hand over my head to turn on the bedside light. When my eyes adjust to the glare, I notice the black streaks on the corner of the duvet that I used to wipe my tears. Did I crawl into bed without removing my makeup? I touch my clumpy eyelashes, confirming my suspicions. What did I do last night? It didn't include eating or washing, apparently.

I frown, trying to conjure up the night before, but to no avail. The last thing I recall is going out to the island, seeing those kids, and coming back here to the cabin. Everything else is hazy.

With effort, I sit up in bed and immediately feel heartburn. *Your ninth week,* I hear the doctor saying. *You're in your ninth week. Did you really have no idea?* No, I didn't. It was because I was so tired, I insisted. The constant exhaustion that never seemed to let up no matter how much I slept. That's why I came in. *Well, now we've solved that mystery,* said the doctor, giving me a polite smile. I left without telling her. Without showing her the marks on my thighs.

Cautiously, with one hand supporting my back, I haul myself to my feet. I really should try to go back to sleep, but then I risk being overpowered by another nightmare. Instead, I go to the kitchen for a glass of water, then to the bathroom to pee. I splash water on my eyes and cheeks. When I raise my head and peer into the bathroom mirror, I think at first that I'm looking at my mother. I cringe and take a step back. Then I notice the dark shadow on my throat. I place my hand over it and turn away so I won't have to look anymore. How alike are we, Mama and I? Could this have been her? If so, what would she have done?

I sink down onto the toilet lid. Mama . . . She called a few more times, but when I saw the familiar number on the display, I didn't answer. Because what is there to say to each other? Nothing. Maybe, to be honest, she feels the same way I do. At any rate, she hasn't left any more messages.

Other than my mother's sporadic attempts, I've had no calls these past few days. No one. I lean forward, wrapping my arms around myself. *Alone. Always so alone.* Then I straighten up, forcing myself to lift my chin. Why would anybody contact me? I'm on vacation, after all.

I haven't called anyone either. Except for Alex. Even though I've repeatedly told myself it's pointless, I keep trying to phone him. Not that I expect him to answer. Not really. By now, I've more or less accepted the fact that he's never going to pick up. That his phone is someplace where no one can hear it ringing.

Finally, I leave the bathroom and tiptoe through the dark. Like an intruder, a stranger. I don't belong here. The cabin seems to know that, as if the walls have come alive and are anxiously leaning toward me. Anxious or hostile. I approach the living room. In the dim light, it looks different, with menacing shadows lurking along the walls, dark figures huddled in the corners. Quickly I reach out for the switch and the room is instantly bathed in light. The hunched and threatening shadows take the shapes of furniture. The same sagging sofa, low coffee table, and mismatched armchairs as usual.

In the big windows facing the deck and yard, I see a mirror image of the room. Like its own illuminated universe, enveloped in darkness. I see the lighting fixture on the ceiling and the worn-out furniture. I can even make out the abstract paintings on the walls. And in the middle of the room, I see myself, my own reflection. A blurry figure wearing a white nightgown, and two dark, tense patches where the eyes should be. And then I see her too. The other one.

I can tell from the shape that it's a woman. But she's thinner than me, more angular. And though I'm standing in the glare of the light, she is cloaked in darkness. I stare at her, realizing who she is. She's me. A younger, innocent version of me. She's the girl who was left behind when Papa disappeared, the young woman I was before Alex. For a brief moment, the image of my young self in the windowpane seems real, and somehow reassuring.

Then my mind wakes up. *Look around you,* it says. I obey. The furniture, the paintings, the room are all brightly lit. I am too. But that woman, the other, is visible only as a dark shape. It's because she's not standing under a light. She isn't here in this living room. She's standing outside. On the deck. Looking in.

22

I was always the spectator. The one who stood outside and looked in, who eavesdropped whenever Mama cried on the phone to Ruth, who secretly listened to Mama and Papa when they fought. But on that night, the last night, I finally became a participant. Instead of tiptoeing back to my own room, I went into my parents' room, drawn by a force stronger than any I'd ever experienced in my eight years of life.

"I know what you did to Greta. Hit your own child? How could you?"

The hurled accusation carried me back to the event I'd tried so hard to suppress. I had been urged not to speak of it. Now it was suddenly a weapon in my parents' battle. Mulle stayed on the floor where I'd dropped him. They were still arguing. But the slap, the fact that one of them had raised a hand to their daughter, was no longer the focus. Now the fight was about something else, someone else.

How quickly my parents had moved on, how easily they'd left behind my shock, pain, and humiliation. Everything I'd been forced to bear was now reduced to only a few seconds of their time and attention. As I stood there in the hallway, emotions flooded over me, took possession of me. I was—there's only one word for it. I was furious.

It took a while before they noticed me. Or rather, when they noticed, it was already too late. Papa was too busy flinging truths in Mama's face to pay any attention to me. Mama had partially turned away. I saw her stony face gradually dissolve until only a gaping mouth and two desperate eyes remained. Even then, Papa kept at it, spewing more poison, firing off more damaging shots.

I stood there, staring at them, and at that moment, something happened, something that changed my worldview. My father. The man who gave me lovely presents and played with me, who said I was sweet and roughhoused with me in the kitchen while he made breakfast. That father was still there somewhere, under the layers of scorn, lies, and betrayal. But I couldn't see him anymore. The man sitting on the sill was somebody else. A horrible man. A cruel man. Someone who tormented Mama. Who made her life hell. And when I thought again about that slap, I had a different feeling inside.

I took a step forward and joined my parents in their violent shadow play. Who made the first move? Who did what? *It escapes me.*

Afterward, I sat in my room and waited. Numb from shock and shame. The paramedics came and went. The police came and went. Before they left, I heard them say to Mama that it would be good if she asked someone to come over and stay with her, that they would gladly call someone for her. I didn't need to hear my mother's reply to know what she would say. There was no one to call. No one. The uniformed officers closed the door behind them, leaving me and Mama alone in the apartment. Since Mama was no longer wailing or crying but lying quietly in her room, they probably thought she would take care of me when they were gone. But she didn't come. I sat there alone.

The darkness lasted an eternity. It got light outside and then dark again. And suddenly, finally, Ruth was standing in the doorway. She said a few words to me, I can't remember what exactly. Then she went to stand in front of the closed door to what was now only Mama's room. I saw her back straighten as she took in a deep breath and knocked. I couldn't hear what they said to each other in there. But after a while, Ruth came back out, pale as a ghost. She ran past my room, gave me a horrified look, and disappeared. That was the last time I saw her.

A little while later, Mama appeared in front of me, leaning on the doorjamb. I blinked. I could hardly believe it was true. Finally, she was here with me again. Moving stiffly, she came over and took me in her arms. I closed my eyes, knowing what would come next. We would talk. We would talk for a long time about guilt and remorse, about responsibility and reconciliation. About justice. And about punishment. I dreaded it. I was already crying. At the same time, I understood there was no avoiding it. There was no other way.

"So," whispered Mama. "It's over now. We will move on, you and I. And we'll stick together. You can count on me."

I waited, but that was all she said. Surprised, I raised my head and looked into Mama's eyes. She stared back, her expression somber, until I realized that was all she intended to say. And she didn't expect me to say anything either. What had happened would remain our secret, hers and mine. There would be no request for forgiveness, not here or in any other context. Silently, my mother lifted her hand, palm up, and held it out toward me.

I stared at it, filled with conflicting emotions. As if I were being pushed down and flying free all at once. Weighted down. But also relieved. I was only eight years old, too young to have any choice. Yet I did choose. I placed my hand in Mama's. From that moment on, it was just the two of us. And we would stick together, just like Mama said. At all costs we would stick together.

23

Wispy bright clouds cover the sun, and a light haze hovers over Marhem. I shove open the glass door to the deck and take a good look around before going out in the yard. The grass is damp. It must have rained in the night. It's pointless to look for tracks, but that's what I do all the same. I'm chewing on a stale cracker to counter the nausea. As my body moves around the property, my eyes search the lawn. Yet it's as if I'm watching myself, surprised I can behave so calmly, so normally, considering everything that's happened over the past few days.

Part of me thinks my agitated brain could have easily misinterpreted what I saw last night. That sort of thing happens when a person is under stress. What I saw outside the living-room window could have been a deer, or even the shadow of a tree. But another part of me knows. It knows exactly what I saw, *who* I saw. And somehow that makes me feel relieved rather than scared.

I redo my makeup, applying extra powder to my throat, and manage to eat half a bowl of yogurt. I tear off a piece of paper and start writing a grocery list. *Milk, fruit, bread.* Then I put down the pen and stare at the banal words on the page. If I'm planning to buy food, it must mean

I intend to stay here. The thought leaves me surprisingly unmoved. *All right,* I think. *All right, then that's what I'll do.* I feel something stirring inside me. Something is about to happen. An itching sensation, as if I'm about to slough off my skin. Soon I'll shed the old husk and step forward as my true self. As the person I've always been but have tried to hold back.

My gaze shifts to Smilla's Barbie dolls, which are still lying on the kitchen floor. I note with amusement that one of the blond girls is lying on top of Ken's face, covering his nose and mouth with her body. His arms are stretched up, as if flailing wildly for air. But he's not going to get away. Barbie has him in her power. Closing my eyes for a moment, I take a deep breath, summoning renewed strength. I made a difficult decision. I did the right thing, chose the only possible option. There was no alternative. Then I think about Smilla, and the guilt returns at once. I can't get rid of it that easily. I steel myself, stand up, and cast another glance at the dolls on the floor. *You have to let go of Smilla. You know that in your heart. You have to.*

Slowly, I go back to the living room and over to the window facing the yard. I stand so close that the tip of my nose touches the pane. For a long time, I stare at the spot where the dark figure stood. I stare so hard that my vision finally splinters and blurs. Just like the other day, when I stood in front of the hall mirror, I suddenly see another face, a face that seems to merge with my own. Her eyes and my eyes fuse, and we are staring straight into the darkness inside both of us. The darkness that we share. *She is me. I am her.* Maybe there's something I can do, after all. Maybe it's not too late.

Before I leave the cabin, I go to refill the cat's bowl but suddenly stop. Where is Tirith? He didn't sleep on the bed with me last night. In fact, I haven't seen him all morning, haven't heard his companionable meowing like I usually do. I look in the living room again, but there's no soft ball of fur curled up on the sofa. Then I remember that I put him outside. When was that? I frown. Yesterday? It must have been yesterday. But I can't recall the exact time of day. The hours are all jumbled together, and the more I strain to sort them out, the more they blur, sliding in and out of each other.

On the road outside, it's now impossible to see any marks in the gravel from the nighttime visitor. The rain has washed away all trace. A sheen of rain covers the windshield of my car, and I imagine that someone used their finger to draw a pattern, connecting the drops. A pattern or a greeting. I wish I could take the car, but that's not possible where I'm going. The forest road around the lake is too narrow in places, besides being very bumpy. But my lower back and hips are aching, so walking isn't an option either.

There's a dilapidated shed behind the cabin. Back there, I find things that Alex must have cleared away, intending to throw them out. A rusty watering can, an inflatable wading pool faded from the sun, and a single oar. Leaning against the wall is an old bicycle. I bend down to test the tires. They seem to have enough air, so I roll the bike out to the road, get on, and start pedaling. I pass the same deserted cabins, the same abandoned patio furniture that I saw yesterday. The bicycle creaks and clatters. The closer I get to my goal, the faster my heart is hammering. And it's not just from physical exertion.

I don't really know what I was expecting, but when I reach the spot where I first met those kids, no one is there. For a long time, I simply stand still, wondering what to do next. All my senses are on alert, and I listen intently, but the only thing I hear is the distant roar of heavy traffic. On the other side of the tall, densely packed trees that surround the lake is the highway leading to town. That's nearly impossible to believe from this location, which feels so remote and far away from everything called civilization.

I lean the bike against a tree trunk and cautiously make my way to the ditch where I first saw the girl yesterday. Even though I'm careful, the damp quickly soaks through my sneakers. My sandals with the straps and heels are still back in the front hall of the cabin, and the

T-shirt I have on is old and faded. Marhem is slowly wearing me down, peeling off my armor. Exposing me. My daily practice of putting on mascara and powder and blush will soon be the only routine I have left. Habits. Rituals. A means of fighting back, a desperate effort to keep from losing my grip altogether.

Finally I reach the lake, right where those boys were standing before the girl noticed me, before the boys rushed up to surround me on the road. I shudder, but then quickly brush the memory aside. I can't let the memory stop me. A short distance away, at the water's edge, are two rowboats. Are those the boats I saw moored at the island yesterday? The ones the kids used to row out there? They must be the same ones. I touch my shoulder, feel the tender bruised spot. I flinch when, out of the corner of my eye, I see something move. I catch a glimpse of a shadowy figure among the trees, but when I blink and then look up again, it's gone.

A suffocating pressure builds in my chest. I shouldn't be here. I really shouldn't. And yet I refuse to leave. I move closer until I'm standing next to the boats. One of them is an old wooden flat-bottomed rowboat. The other is more modern, made of plastic and fiberglass. Once upon a time, it must have been white, but now the bow is a dirty gray. The scratched stripes painted on the sides look like they were originally navy blue. Something pulls me even closer, and I peer over the gunwale. The bottom of the boat is filled with a few inches of water, probably from last night's downpour. But the water isn't clear. It's streaked with red. Lying under the seat in the stern is a clotted lump smeared dark red. As big as an aborted fetus.

I lurch back and bump right into a tree. Except it's not a tree. It's a person. I spin around, and there we stand, face-to-face.

"I had a feeling you'd come back," says the girl. "But this has to be the last time."

24

My initial feeling is relief. The same sense of relief I had when I saw the dark figure on the lawn outside the cabin last night. *You're alive. You weren't the one screaming on the island yesterday, you weren't the one they had hurt.* Then she gives me a shove in the chest and I stumble backward. I stare at her, looking at her clenched fists and peering into the trees behind her. The girl seems to read my mind.

"I'm alone," she says. "But you won't be that lucky next time. If you're smart, you'll stay away from here. Don't come back! Leave us alone!"

There's something about her voice. It sounds more anxious than threatening. As if she wants to protect me. And she has lowered her hands. My pulse slows a bit. I have a reason for being here. But first I need to win her trust, show that I'm taking her seriously.

"What are you trying to warn me against? What might happen?"

She snorts. "You don't want to mess with Jorma. You should have realized that by now."

I brush a few stray strands of hair out of my face and study her more closely. I wonder how old she is. Under the dark-colored man's shirt she's wearing, I can't see even a slight swelling of breasts. But that's not really surprising, considering how thin she is.

"Jorma? Is that his name? Your boyfriend?"

A splotchy blush colors the girl's cheeks.

"He's not my . . . We're not exactly . . ."

I wonder whether they're sleeping together. Then I shake my head. Of course they are. I hear a snapping sound from the trees, and I freeze. But no Jorma comes rushing toward us. Not yet. I swallow hard, realizing that it's only a matter of time before he or one of the other boys shows up. I need to hurry if I'm going to say what I've come here to say. It's now or never.

"You don't have to put up with this."

My words surprise her. I watch her blink, then she says:

"What . . . what do you mean?"

She pretends not to understand, but I can see her looking at my throat. She can't help staring. In her eyes, I see her answer. I see the truth. I take a step closer but restrain myself from reaching out to take hold of her arms.

"What's your name?"

"Greta," she says at last.

Greta? The same name. That too. I summon my courage and go on.

"Listen to me now, Greta. If he treats you badly . . . Don't let him get away with it. You have to strike back, free yourself."

The corner of her eye twitches.

"I'm not—" she begins.

But I'm too impatient to let her finish. I have no time for excuses.

"You can say what you like, but in your heart you know that you're looking for a way out. You're looking for someone who can help you. That's why you came to my cabin. That's why you stood in the yard outside the window last night. Because you know that I'm like you."

I instantly see that I've made a mistake; I've gone too far. Until now the girl has barely moved as she listened, but from one second to the next her face darkens.

"That's not why," she snarls.

Somehow things have taken a wrong turn. I've said too much or said something wrong. The fragile connection between us has crumbled. But I can't stop myself. I'm still filled with the thought of what we have in common, convinced that she needs me.

"I'm on your side," I blurt out. "Don't you realize that? You and I, we have a lot—"

"Who the hell do you think you are? We are not on the same side!"

She shouts so loud that I fall silent and take a step back. For a moment, I think I see her face contort in a grimace of pain and shame, but then it's gone. Replaced by a hard and impenetrable mask. She looks away. Her arm shoots out, straight and tense. She seems agitated as she points at something right behind me.

"Jorma knows now! He knows you were the one who did it!"

I turn to look where she's pointing, toward the boats. My eyes are drawn to the smeared lump and the blood in the bottom of the newer boat. An icy cold spreads through my body.

"Did what?" I ask, my voice hoarse.

"We know you've been on the island. We're the only ones who go out there. So it must have been you."

Everything is shimmering before my eyes. I don't reply. Because what is there to say? I stand there, feeling how it's seeping out of me. All my self-confidence and strength. The girl puts her hands on her hips.

"Did you go there alone? Out to the island, I mean. Were you alone, or were there others?"

Her voice now has a commanding ring to it. As if this were an interrogation. And in a way, it is. I realize it makes no difference what I say. My throat tightens, and I take a step back.

"No . . . or, yes. It was me and my husband and my . . . my . . ."

I struggle to finish the sentence, but I can't. Dizziness is making the ground spin under my feet. The lies are swarming over each other, slithering around my body and threatening to pull me down. I've lied ever since we came here to Marhem. To the girl and her gang, to the man in the brown house, to the police. Even I have no idea why. But it doesn't matter; the reason is of no consequence. The only important thing is that it can't go on. I can't lie anymore. Alex is not my husband. And Smilla is not my daughter.

"There were three of us who went out to the island. But the other two . . ."

Not another lie. Not to her. The girl is waiting. But when I don't go on, she gets impatient.

"What? What about the other two?"

How do I explain? *They didn't come back. They disappeared.* Slowly, very slowly, I keep backing away from the water and the girl, moving toward the forest road and my bicycle. But my young namesake follows. Again she shoves me hard in the chest.

"Confess! I already know what you did. We all know."

Then I turn around. And run. As fast as I can, cutting between the trees and clambering over the ditch. Back up on the forest road, I grimace with pain and nausea, but I don't allow myself to pause or rest. I grab the bike and jump on. The girl makes no attempt to hold me back. As I ride away from there, I hear her yelling after me.

"Jorma will make sure you're punished."

At that moment, when I hear those words, something clicks inside me. Something important is making its way through the haze that envelops my consciousness. A realization. Revenge. That's the thought pounding in my head. He's out for revenge. He's going to make sure I'm punished. But Jorma isn't the *he* I'm thinking about.

25

It was never a secret that Alex was married. From early on in our relationship, he was open about the fact that he had a wife and daughter in his life. It wasn't something that bothered me. On the contrary. Even though I'd been reluctant to allow anyone to get close, it seemed just as unthinkable to let go when Alex came into my life.

Before I knew it, I'd told both my mother and Katinka about him. Mama had asked me so many times, with a hopeful look in her eyes, whether there was anyone special in my life. But she wasn't pleased when she heard about Alex. Did I let slip the fact that he was already taken? Or did Mama ask questions that led her to that conclusion? I'm not really sure. All I remember is her reaction.

How could you, Greta? How on earth could you?

I knew what she was thinking—that I was my father's daughter, that I was following in his reprehensible footsteps. But I wasn't responsible for Alex's infidelity. I owed nothing to that faceless woman who sat somewhere, waiting for him to come home. Truth be told, I respectfully didn't give a shit about her. Just like I didn't give a shit about Mama's disapproval.

Katinka was also skeptical, but she promised to share my joy if I was happy. *Happy,* I thought one evening, a month after the start of my relationship with Alex. *Am I happy?* I turned my head to look at him lying next to me on the mattress.

"Shouldn't we talk more? Get to know each other? Isn't that what people do?"

He grinned at me.

"If you want to," he said. "So tell me something about yourself. Something really shameful."

My throat closed up. Something shameful? *Papa.* The subject never to be discussed. No one had ever been able to get the truth out of me about what happened. It was the reason I'd spent my whole life keeping people at arm's length. But here I was now, with a man who claimed to see me, really see me. And suddenly I heard myself telling Alex about that night. About the open window, about Papa falling into eternity. When I came to the end, something made me stop, keep the most crucial details to myself. But I'd told him enough.

"I think you're a little crazy, sweetheart. Not exactly right in the head."

Alex laughed, but I could see in his eyes that he was serious. And he was probably right. After that, I gradually gave up any hope for emotional closeness. I had someone at my side. That was enough. We didn't need to know everything about each other.

Then came the night when Alex pressed my naked body against the windowpane.

Don't ever leave me. That's what it said on the card that came with the flowers the next day. It might have been a plea. Or a command. No matter what, I didn't leave. I couldn't stand the thought of being alone again. Instead, I placed myself in Alex's hands, allowed him to lead me further into the dark. Pain slowly crept into our relationship.

But still I didn't leave. I continued to cling to him. Alex led and I followed. Until the path led down into the abyss.

I hear a beeping in my pocket. I take a deep breath, look around in a daze. Where am I? I take in my surroundings, realize that I'm sitting in my car in a half-empty parking lot outside a small grocery store. How did I get here? I must have driven, of course, but I don't remember doing that. Then I recall my encounter with the girl, the bike ride through the woods back to the cabin, the lactic acid in my legs, the taste of blood in my mouth. The fateful shouts about revenge and punishment resounding through the forest and inside my head. I remember the fear, can still feel it tingling in my fingertips and churning in my stomach. But it's not only fear. It's more than that. It's a sense of rebellion, the desire to stand up and confront the enemy. Finally that feeling has awakened inside me. That's why I'm here. To take action.

The beeping sound in my pocket again. I take out my cell. A text message from Katinka. *Hope you guys are fine. Thinking of you.* Only two sentences, but heavily charged with meaning.

As time passed, and my relationship with Alex changed, as I accepted more, asked for more, Katinka was always there with her silent, searching eyes. When I started calling in sick more often, she would ask me how I was really feeling. She was the only one who noticed there was something strange about the way I was walking that day. Or at least the only one who asked me outright.

"Why are you limping?"

"I'm not limping."

"Maybe not. But you're moving kind of strange. Sort of carefully. As if you hurt. What happened?"

She fixed her gaze on me. I pressed my lips together, tried to meet her eyes but had to make do with looking at the wall. Katinka slowly nodded. As if she understood something important. Then she told me I should go and talk to someone. I gave a start and asked what she meant. She didn't reply, didn't even say what I knew she was referring to.

"What do you mean?" I persisted. "What exactly do you think I need to talk about?"

Part of me wanted to hear her say it out loud, wanted her to make it real, everything that I wasn't able to express.

"You're not yourself anymore," Katinka told me. "The way you're limping. And you're always tired. You should see someone."

"Who?"

I expected her to suggest some sort of therapist. When I closed my eyes I pictured a mane of blond hair and felt a firm grip on my wrist. *Things are going to get worse for you. And you risk being knocked off balance.* But Katinka wasn't thinking about a psychologist. She had something else in mind.

"Maybe you should see a doctor at the clinic."

"Okay," I said. "You're right. I *am* tired. I'll make an appointment."

And I did. A few days later, I went to the clinic. Outside, the sun was shining and everyone seemed to be wearing shorts and light dresses. I had on long pants. The image of the blond psychologist again flickered through my mind. Cardigans and jackets in the middle of summer. I'd always found that strange. Now I dressed the same way myself. All covered up.

A short time later, I was ushered into the office of a woman wearing a white coat. I sat down in the chair in front of her desk. It took a while before I said anything. I waited, letting her study me in silence. I secretly wished that she'd just look at me and know, without me having to say a word. But her expression was so inquisitive that I was finally forced to open my mouth. Hesitantly, I told her about the fatigue, then answered her questions obediently, though evasively. When she ordered tests, I allowed the nurse to stick a needle in my arm to draw blood, and I peed in the container they handed me.

Afterward, we again sat across from each other. The doctor tilted her head to one side as she peered at me. *Ask to look at my thighs,* I thought. *Tell me I have to leave him.* But she did neither. Instead, she explained that I was pregnant. Nine weeks. Had I really not suspected?

I get out of the car and go inside the grocery store, which is housed in a low brick building. An elderly man is standing at the checkout counter closest to the doors, reading a newspaper. When I come in, he looks up and says hello. I pick up a basket and aimlessly stroll the aisles. It's a sleepy country store, and the selection is accordingly limited. I could have driven a little farther, to the town where I was yesterday, but I don't dare go back there. I don't want to go anywhere near the police station and risk being recognized.

I feel heat rise to my cheeks when I think about the phone conversation with the female police officer. What a fuss I'd caused. And yet it could be worse, much worse. If the police discover that two people named Alex and Smilla have actually disappeared, and they also know that I'm lying about my relationship to them . . . It wouldn't look good. Not at all.

In one of the aisles, I run into two old ladies who look amazingly alike. Maybe they're sisters. The kind who have never married, who have stayed together in this slumbering town and shared a different sort of life.

They give me a cautious smile, the way you'd smile at an eccentric stranger, as we pass each other. I strain to return the smile. *It's not my fault,* I want to shout at them. *I just did what I was told.*

I had asked Alex how he intended to introduce me if we met anyone while we were in Marhem. Back home, we never went out; we just stayed indoors, at my place. No movie theaters, no restaurants, not even walks in the evening. We never talked about the reason, but I assumed it was because of *her.* The town was small enough that if we went out we might run into someone who knew either her or Alex. Up to that point, the world that he and I had shared was no bigger than my bedroom.

Now we were suddenly going to step forward into an unknown universe. We would go away, spend our vacation together. I didn't ask Alex what he'd said at home, but I guessed he'd conjured up some sort of business trip. He was a sales rep, always traveling, which meant she should have accepted the explanation. His wife. Because he did have a wife, after all.

So how was he planning to introduce me, I wondered. How did he want me to introduce myself? Alex shrugged at my queries, didn't think it mattered because we weren't likely to run into anyone. At least no one he knew. But I insisted.

"But what if someone asks?" I said. "*What if?* I want to know who I am. Who I'm supposed to be."

That caught his attention. He stared at me for a long time, an unreadable look in his eyes.

"You're my woman," he finally said firmly. "If anyone asks, that's what you should tell them."

So that's what I did. The man in the brown house, the police, the kids—that's what I let all of them believe. That I was the one Alex was married to. But it was different with Smilla. Nobody had urged me to call her my daughter, yet I'd allowed her to become part of the charade. It had happened so naturally. It was almost alarmingly easy. Little Smilla, who had the same princess dreams I'd once had, and the same father figure—playful and fun as a dad, worthless and unscrupulous as a spouse. Smilla, who was connected to me through the child I now carried inside.

"Your sister or brother," I whisper with a shiver as I stand in front of the grocery store cooler.

For a long time, I stare at the containers of milk, butter, yogurt, and eggs. Then I glance down at the red basket I'm holding. It's still empty.

In the back of my mind, I know that getting in the car and driving here to shop for groceries is just a pretext. What I'm looking for is something else entirely. But what? The two old ladies are approaching. Quickly, I take two cartons of yogurt from the shelf and place them in my basket. I hope now I look like any other ordinary customer. Normal. At least outwardly.

I move to the back of the store, trying to keep it together. I put some fruit in a plastic bag, which I place in the basket along with a loaf of light rye bread. Suddenly I find myself in front of a shelf of diapers and baby food. And I'm staring straight into the memory of how Alex reacted when he heard I was pregnant. *Have you made an appointment?* I remember that afterward he took his time finishing his dinner, that he seemed to be chewing very calmly and carefully. Yet there was something alarming about the way his jaws kept grinding back and forth. Something that indicated suppressed rage. Or is that just my interpretation in hindsight?

After he'd cleaned his plate, he pushed it aside and left the room to get something. He came back holding a black silk tie. Then he took off his jacket and handed both items to me.

"Put these on over your panties. Nothing else. Wait for me in the bedroom."

One more try, just one last time. Maybe that's what I was thinking. Maybe that's why I repressed the memory of the pain in my thighs, the pain that had eventually faded and yet had etched silent, indelible traces inside my body. In any case, I did as Alex wanted. I got undressed, slipped the tie around my neck, and waited. Then he came into the bedroom. And closed the door to the world.

It took a long time for me to fall asleep that night, and when I finally did, it was a restless and fitful slumber. A short time later I woke up, either from pain or because of sounds outside. The rumbling car engine, the loud screams. I lay there, listening to Alex carry Smilla inside, noting how he turned on lights and put her to bed in the room next to ours. Through the wall, I heard him talking to her, his words quiet and reassuring.

I didn't get out of bed, but I was definitely wide awake. And it was at that moment I made up my mind. Actually, it was more of a realization than a decision. *This has to stop.*

There was a clarity in those words, a feeling that I'd been missing for a long time. I had to do what must be done. It made me feel both heavy and light. There was no doubt in my mind whatsoever.

I reach out and touch a baby bottle, then a sippy cup with a Winnie-the-Pooh decal. *Is this what I'm looking for? Is this why I'm here? No.* I lower my hands. My body moves away. I'm almost at the checkout counter, but I haven't found what I'm looking for. Something is buried in my consciousness, mocking me, hidden. I put a bag of cat food in my basket, and then I'm in the section for home and garden supplies. My eyes land on a medium-sized ax on one of the lower shelves, and something clicks.

I set down the basket and squat in front of the tools on display. My ears are ringing as I reach out and grab the handle. I pick up the ax, weigh it in my hand. It's substantial for its size.

I've never held an ax before. Yet the feel of the grooved plastic handle seems so familiar, completely natural. How can that be? I lean forward and read what it says on a sign fastened to the shelf. "Multifunctional. Case-Hardened Steel. Lifetime Guarantee." I close my eyes a second.

Then I carefully touch the blade with my fingertips. The feeling prompts a bass note to resonate through my whole body. After it fades, a familiar echo starts up. *In the worst-case scenario, that sort of state of mind could have very unfortunate consequences. For you, or for those close to you.* I practically fling the ax away. What the blond psychologist warned me about—is that what's happening now? Have I reached a point where I can no longer predict my actions or control what I do? Have I reached that point—or have I already passed it? *Oh, Smilla!*

I cover my eyes and rock desperately back and forth as I crouch there on the floor of the grocery store. We hadn't planned to bring her with us to Marhem. Unforeseen circumstances prompted her nighttime arrival. *The one who stayed and the one who left.* And now . . . What is it I'm trying to tell myself now? That unforeseen circumstances are also behind her disappearance? I take my hands away from my eyes and again fix my gaze on the object in front of me. I need to be realistic. Once again, I reach out for the ax.

I'm approaching the highway exit for Marhem when my phone starts ringing. *Katinka,* I think. I didn't answer her text, so now she's calling to see if I'm okay. I remember what Mama said the first day after they went missing, when I was still taking her calls. *Katinka is worried about you.* Feeling tense, I pull out my phone. But it's not Katinka's number on the display.

My other hand jerks the steering wheel so hard that the car swerves across the lane. I shriek before regaining control. Up ahead, I see a turnout, a waiting area for the buses that travel the highway back and forth to town. I cast a frantic glance in the rearview mirror, but there's no bus in sight on the stretch of road behind me. Clutching the wheel with both hands, I pull into the bus stop and brake, a little too hard.

My phone is still ringing, and I stare at it wild eyed. No, it's not Katinka's number. There are no digits on the display. Only a name. A very familiar one.

"Alex," I whisper.

My hand picks up the phone. The skin on my palm twinges—it's the wound from the other day, the wound from my own earring. Just before I press the "Answer" button, my eyes shift to the plastic bags on the floor in front of the passenger seat. The bags containing the groceries I bought. Yogurt, fruit, bread. And the ax. The multifunctional tool, with a blade of tempered steel and a lifetime guarantee.

I take a deep breath and answer, trying unsuccessfully to make my voice sound normal.

"Hello? Alex? Where are you? What happened?"

I hear a scraping sound on the other end.

"Hello?" I shout again, a little more firmly this time. "Can you hear me?"

Still no answer. All I hear is a rushing sound. Then total silence. I take the phone away from my ear and stare at it. I try again, shouting Alex's name louder and louder. But the connection is dead. There's no one there.

26

It's gotten so dark. The last bit of strength has seeped out of me; there's nothing left. Nothing to hold me up. I can't get up, can't do anything. All I can do is lie here in the dark and look around. It's all so familiar, yet it seems different now. Changed. Ruined.

I hear your voice. And if I make a slight effort, I can see you in my mind, picture your face and your body. But I can't penetrate into your consciousness, get hold of who you are. What thoughts are racing through your mind right now? Are you confused? Lonely? Resigned? Or is there some solace, hope? Do you believe things will get better? That everything will work out in the end? Do you ever think of me? Answer me!

How do I go on? What can I do? Without me, you are nothing. *Words that exposed and humiliated me, made me shrink and cower. But now . . . now I feel something in my body, feel it growing and getting closer. Preparing to claw its way out. Soon I will get up. I'll stand determined and erect. I will leave what has been, put it all behind me. The future is waiting. She is waiting.*

Soon it will grow light. Soon I will go to meet her.

And you'll be left alone in the shadows. May they swallow you up.

27

The key. Where is the damn key? I dig through my purse, have to put down my grocery bags to search properly. The top of one of the bags falls open, and I see the black handle of the ax I just bought. Then I remember. The key isn't in my purse. I just thought it was, out of habit from back in town. Here in Marhem the routines are different.

When I'm again standing at the bottom of the steps, I reach my hand underneath to get the key from its hiding place and then feel a burning sensation on my back. An intense feeling that I'm being watched spreads through me. Am I just imagining things, or is that the sound of twigs snapping somewhere beyond the tall arborvitae in front of the cabin? Is someone there? I start to shake and almost drop the key.

Without turning around—I refuse to give in to fear—I walk back up the steps. I stick the key in the lock, give it a turn, and press down on the door handle. But the door doesn't open. Two more times, I grab the handle and pull the door toward me, but nothing happens. It's still locked, even though I just unlocked it. Or did I? With trembling hands, I try again. Put the key in the lock, give it a turn, and then press down on the handle. Now the door opens easily.

Quickly, I pull it shut behind me and stand in the entryway for a moment, leaning against the wall, panting. Was the door even locked to begin with? Did I forget to lock it? Surely I remembered to lock up when I drove to the grocery store, although I have no clear memory of doing so. But how often does anyone recall those kinds of things that they do more or less automatically?

Was someone out there? If so, who could it be? Jorma? Again I feel the knife jabbing under my chin. Jorma probably wouldn't have settled for spying on me from the bushes. But maybe it was some of his followers. Maybe they found out which cabin is mine. Maybe they have nothing better to do than to prowl around outside, both nonchalant and eager, waiting for something to happen. I stare at the closed front door. *In that case,* I think, *their wish will soon be granted.* Something *is* about to happen.

My tongue sticks to the roof of my mouth as I head for the kitchen with my bags. I stow everything in the fridge and cupboards, all except for the ax, which I leave in the bag so I can pretend not to see it. The other option is to pretend it's intended for yard work. Deep inside, I want to hold on to the belief that I'm the same person I was before we came to Marhem. A person who would never even think of buying an ax, let alone consider it a weapon.

It's already afternoon, and my stomach is growling. I should eat something, but I have no appetite, nor can I settle down to eat in peace. So I make do with a couple of glasses of juice. I'm standing at the kitchen counter, drinking the juice, when I again have that prickling sensation on my back. I turn around slowly, and that's when I notice her. The doll. Five of the six kitchen chairs are neatly pushed under the table, but the sixth one has been pulled out. And on the chair sits Smilla's big baby doll with the eyes that open and close. Her chubby arms are raised over her head, and her cornflower-blue eyes are staring at me. I clutch the glass in my hand. My pulse, which had just begun to ease, quickens again. Was she sitting there this morning? Or yesterday? My phone rings.

On trembling legs, I run to the entryway, where I left my purse. My stomach is knotting as I stand there with the phone in my hand, staring at the display. The same name as before. The phone is slick with sweat as I press it to my ear.

"Alex? Is that you?"

But there's no one on the phone this time either, at least no one who responds. After shouting Alex's name several times and hearing only the echo of my own hoarse voice, I end the call.

Shaken, I stare at myself again in the hall mirror. My mind is flying in all directions, trying to contain what refuses to be captured, trying not to slip or lose hold. I think about the screeching tires and the loud screams outside the cabin on our first night here. I think about how, on returning to the cabin after Alex and Smilla disappeared, I couldn't find my phone and how it finally showed up, neatly covered on Alex's side of the bed. I think about the trouble I had opening the front door, and the possibility that it was unlocked all day. And then I think about Smilla's doll in the kitchen, about its wide-open, staring eyes, its little mouth shaped in a silent scream, and its arms reaching up in a plea for help.

I stagger toward the bedroom, realizing I need to lie down. When I reach the doorway, my eyes fall on the lacy red bra still draped over a chair, and I pause. I bought the bra when Alex suggested—or rather, told me—that we would be driving to Marhem for a few days. We would go together, just the two of us. It was short notice, but I managed to get a few days off. At lunchtime, I ran out to buy new underwear. Not because I really wanted to, or because I needed anything new, but because I felt like it was expected of me. I also bought a tie for Alex, a black silk tie. I gave it to him when he came over later that night. He stared at it for a long time, letting it tenderly slide through his fingers.

"I'll bring it to the cabin," he said at last.

We ate dinner, and afterward he stroked me languidly, provocatively. He made me hope, made me relax. This time, we would make love without pain, without any unpleasant surprises. Alex was good at what he was doing, and I gasped as I arched toward the ceiling. But just as I was about to reach orgasm, he moved his hand, grabbed the flesh on the inside of my thigh, and pinched as hard as he could. I screamed. Then he did the same thing on my other leg. And this time, he didn't just pinch. He twisted my skin and the underlying fat and muscles until they burned. The pain was so extreme that everything went black, and I lost all sense of time and place. My body was lifted up and turned over. For a moment, my face was pressed against the mattress as he mounted me. I remember thinking: *Who are you really?* Then it was over.

Afterward, Alex's breath was hot in my ear when he whispered about the thin line between pain and pleasure. He said he wanted us to explore that more. A few days later, I was sitting in the clinic, wearing long pants, talking about how inexplicably tired I felt. And then I heard the news that changed everything. *Your ninth week. Did you really have no idea?* My world was turned upside down. I didn't know what to do, so I did nothing. Made no decisions. Took no action. And suddenly, the day arrived, the day of our departure for Marhem.

I can't get myself to go into the bedroom. The lacy red bra mercilessly leads my thoughts to the black silk tie, and my aversion is so strong that I feel faint. Where is it now? I haven't seen it since our first night here, but it must be somewhere, neatly rolled or hung up. Probably in the bedroom, in Alex's wardrobe.

I stumble back and turn instead to Smilla's room. Toys are scattered everywhere, reminding me of the girl who slept and played in this room so recently. But when I lie down on her bed and again bury my face in the pillow, I no longer smell the warm, sweet scent of her hair. She's far away from here now, far away.

"I'm sorry," I murmur into the pillowcase. "I'm sorry it turned out like this."

The image of pale legs underneath a bush flashes through my mind, but I push it away and manage to replace it with a different picture. Now Smilla floats into view, flying into the kitchen in Alex's strong arms. Then he sets her down on the chair across from me, and she looks at him lovingly as he fixes breakfast. It's our first morning together, hers and mine. And our last. If I'd known that beforehand, would I have acted differently, made other choices?

What did Smilla think about my presence there at the breakfast table? Did she see the mark that was beginning to appear on my throat and wonder what it was? Or was she too young to understand such things, too young to come to any conclusions about her father and this strange woman wearing a nightgown? I turn over in bed and stare at the one remaining eye of Smilla's teddy bear, which is lying against the wall. The truth is, I'm not even sure she saw me. I mean, she was aware I was sitting there. But she didn't *see* me, not really. She was too wrapped up in something else. Every time she opened her mouth that morning, it was about herself and Alex. Smilla and Papa. Papa and Smilla. Her love for him was palpable.

As I sat on the other side of the table and saw her watching him with adoration in her eyes, I felt the jealousy growing stronger inside me. I felt left out. I wanted what they had. And the decision I'd made during the night solidified. As soon as we were done eating, I took Alex aside and told him. I had made up my mind. I was planning to leave him. He patted my cheek, but not hard or angrily. More distracted.

"No," he said. "No, you won't."

Then he left me there, my body heavy as lead. Because I understood what his words meant. I thought the hard part was deciding to leave Alex, that once I'd made the decision, the rest would be easy. Only then did I realize how tightly Alex had spun his web around me. I was entangled in so many ingenious threads that there was no way out. What I planned was impossible.

I couldn't leave Alex. He would never allow that, simply because he was the one who controlled our relationship. On the day he tired of me, we would part, but not a second before. And if I did try to leave . . . He would come after me, bring me back. He knew where I worked, where I lived. He knew everything about my life. He was my life. I had to find some other means, another way out. But how? What?

I get up and straighten the duvet on Smilla's bed. As if someone might sleep here tonight. As if I actually think she's coming back. When I look up, my eyes are drawn to the window. I glimpse something move on the other side of the pane. My throat closes up as I take the few steps over to the window and pull down the blind. A deer, I tell myself. This time it must have been a deer.

28

It's dark when the shrill ringing of my phone yanks me out of the fog of sleep. *Who would call me in the middle of the night?* I wonder blearily. The next second I'm wide awake and reaching for my cell. Again, it's Alex's name on the display. Again there's only silence on the other end. I shout hello several times, but no one answers.

Either the person on the phone is unable to speak, or the call isn't intended to convey a message in words. Maybe it means something else. A cry for help. Or a threat. How am I supposed to know which? A disconsolate feeling surges inside of me. Along with another feeling, strong and insistent.

"Go to hell!" I bellow into the phone, before I abruptly end the call.

I'm surprised at the force of my anger and frustration. But then it ebbs away, replaced by guilt. Again I picture those pale legs sticking out from under a bush and imagine the lifeless body of the girl beneath the foliage. This time it's not as easy to shake off the image. *Smilla!*

Automatically, I reach out my hand and run it over the duvet, looking for Tirith's soft body. I need him close to me; I need the solace that only another living creature can offer. But there's no cat lying on the bed. My disappointment soon gives way to something else, something darker. When did I last see him? My memory takes me back to the moment I came inside after the failed visit to the police station.

I picture Tirith licking the wound on the palm of my hand. And then . . . then I threw him out. It was an impulsive act, based on a sudden aversion to his name. I haven't seen him since. Busy with other things, I hardly gave Tirith a thought, and he's been wandering around outside, cast out and alone. Defenseless in the face of the dangers hovering over Marhem.

I jump out of bed, and nausea assails me like an enraged animal. I make it to the bathroom just in time. Leaning over the toilet bowl, I expel what little is left inside my stomach. I've hardly eaten anything over the past few days, just a little yogurt and toast. The heartburn is worse than ever, as is the throbbing in the small of my back. I place my hand over my stomach and press down lightly.

"We need to go and look for your sister's cat," I murmur. I need to find Tirith, even if it's the last thing I do.

I put on a sweater and a pair of loose pants. The night air is chilly. And who knows how long I might have to be outside? I don't intend to give up until I've found my black-and-white pal. I'm not coming back until I have him safely in my arms.

In the hall wardrobe, I find an old, thin anorak. It's gray with pink trim. I pull it over my head, trying not to think about who it might belong to, the fact that it's probably *hers*. I stand there in the dim light, staring at my own reflection in the mirror. Pale, with no makeup, wearing practical but far from attractive clothing. A completely different woman from the one who arrived here a couple of days ago.

Layer after layer of polish and external trappings and ingrained patterns have been scraped off me. This is what is left. This is the person I've become.

There's a continuous line running through time, from that night when Papa fell out the window on the ninth floor until the moment when Alex and Smilla disappeared on the island. It's not a straight line. It keeps twisting and turning until it takes the shape of a circle. And it's at the spot where the ends meet that I am now standing. The person I've always been. The one who came out of the shadows, the one who has returned to the shadows.

I'm halfway out the door when I realize I'm missing something. Without taking off my shoes, I go into the kitchen and find the plastic bag on the floor. The ax is sticking out of the bag. I grab the black handle in both hands and lift it up, holding it out in front of my body. As I pass through the entryway again, I cast another glance in the mirror, prepared to see myself looking clumsy and awkward. But I have a steady, firm grip on the ax. I'm holding it with great determination. It looks like I've done this before.

I go outside, not knowing where I'm headed. I walk without thinking about where I set my feet or what's around me. Only when I feel branches brushing against my cheeks do I realize I'm in the woods. Not near the lake, not on the forest road, but deep among the trees. It's still dark here even though the sky is tinged with yellow and pink. I hear a twig snap somewhere behind me, and I spin around.

"Tirith?"

But I don't hear any meowing, and there's no lithe black-and-white figure coming toward me between the trees. On one level, I'm aware that it's wrong for me to be here, that I'll never find a cat in the middle of the woods. At the same time, all I can think about is the guilt I feel toward Smilla. About what I've subjected her to, how she became an innocent victim because of me. Nausea is churning in my intestines like a clenched fist, but I refuse to give up. Looking for Tirith is the least I can do.

"Here, kitty, kitty. Tirith!"

I go one way, then the other, first forward, then back, keeping my eyes fixed on the ground. *Where could he be? Where does a cat go?* I shake my head. What if Alex had voluntarily allowed me to leave? Would everything have turned out differently? That's something I'll never know. A big branch suddenly snaps back and slaps me right in the face.

The pain sends white flashes through my mind, burning everything away. When my vision clears, the ax is lying on the ground. I bend down and pick it up. My cheek is stinging, and I wipe off something sticky that turns my palm red. The same hand that I stabbed with my earring a little while ago.

A little while ago? I stare in surprise at the delicate bright-pink skin on the spot where I stuck myself. No puncture. No blood. Is it healed already? How long ago was it that I actually got cut? It feels like it just happened, but was it yesterday? Or even the day before? Was it before or after the well? I frown. *The well?* Yes, the well out on the island. *There's no well on the island.* Then what was it I pictured when I stared down at Lake Malice's dark water? *No, he never leaned over any well.* But did I cut myself on the earring before or after my hands shoved his shoulder blades?

Every time a clear thought is about to take shape in my head, it evaporates. Somewhere inside me a voice is shouting, as if in protest, but it's so far away I can't tell if it's real or imaginary. I'm fumbling blindly, both here among the trees and in my own consciousness. The only thing left is the sense that I'm searching for something. There's something I need to find. Something or someone.

I run through the woods, pushing my body to its limit. I hold out the ax in front of me like a shield, an invocation against evil. The only sound is the rustling of the anorak and my own ragged breathing. I don't know how long I've been out here or what direction I'm heading in. Maybe I'm going in circles. Finally, I see light among the tree trunks, and the crazed beast spinning inside my head gradually calms down.

I stop to catch my breath. The world is again clear, at least with regard to the more tangible details. There's no sign of Tirith. Or of Alex and Smilla. Of course not. My skin is prickling; my head is spinning. The truth is right there in front of me, hidden under the ax. Now and then, light glints off the blade, like fish scales underwater. But each time I reach out my hands, it slips out of my grasp, as slippery as a fish.

I don't allow myself to rest for long before resuming my aimless wandering. Find Tirith. Find Smilla. Find Alex. As soon as I find Alex it will be over. If only I can find him, it will finally be over. Sweat trickles down my face and my back. But the feeling of being the one searching is increasingly replaced by the feeling of being hunted. Silent footsteps creeping behind me. Something that slips behind a tree trunk when I turn around. Maybe it's Alex coming back for revenge. Revenge? For what? Again thoughts whirl haphazardly through my mind. Without meaning, direction, or goal, they break loose. All reason flees. I see what's happening, but I'm helpless to act.

A faint vibration against my thigh brings me to a halt. Even though I hear no sound, I dig the phone out of my pants pocket, but without letting go of the ax. My cell phone. My only link to reality, to the outside world. The thought makes me feel both relieved and uneasy. There's a new text from Katinka. She writes that she's on her way home from some after-party, and she's wondering why I haven't answered her last text. The disjointed phrases and messy syntax indicate she must be drunk.

The phone beeps again, and then again. Katinka sends more texts, one after another. I halfheartedly skim over her reports of cute guys and aching feet. I'm just about to stuff the phone back in my pocket when I suddenly get a text about my mother. Apparently, Mama tried to get hold of me at work again, even though she knows I'm not there.

Upset. Wanted to know where you were. Tried to get me to tell her. Thought I knew.

Is Katinka mad that I didn't tell her where Alex and I were going for vacation? Or is she just stating the facts, that Mama asked her where I was but she couldn't tell her because she doesn't know? I have no idea. I lost the ability to decipher those sorts of normal but unspoken signals between friends long ago. Maybe I never had it. *You should see someone. Maybe you should see a doctor at the clinic.*

So much has happened since that day when Katinka noticed I was having trouble walking because of my thighs. There's an ocean of thoughts and deeds between that day and this one. I have a strong desire to text back, tell her I'm pregnant. She doesn't even know that. But on closer examination, there's really very little she knows about me. I stand still for a moment with my fingers hovering over the keyboard on the display in front of me. But no sensible reply comes to mind.

With my phone back in my pocket, I start walking again. Would it be possible for us to be real friends, Katinka and I? So far I've chosen not to think about that. So far what has governed my relationship with Katinka—as with all my acquaintances before her—is the thought of Mama and the best friend she once had. *It'll never be like with Mama and Ruth. I can't risk getting too close.*

The trees are thinning out up ahead, opening on a small clearing. I stop near the edge, right in front of something low to the ground. My mind conjures up events from long ago, remembering how things played out during the last dramatic period of the friendship between Mama and Ruth. An incident that began with a failed trip to see my maternal grandmother and ended with Papa falling out the bedroom window. Although it actually ended several months earlier, of course, with the slap.

I'm so immersed in my thoughts that at first I don't process the object at my feet. Then my gaze moves down, fixing on something brown and knotty. Two sticks fastened together in an ancient symbol. I stare at the object for a moment before the realization sinks in. A cross. But why . . . ? What . . . ? I take a step back, staring hard, first at the little wooden cross, then at the mound of earth in front of it, then back again. An icy wave washes over me, sweeping away everything else. Leaving behind only the knowledge that this wasn't just any object hidden in this clearing. It was a grave.

Then I hear a rustling very close by, and this time I'm sure. Someone is standing behind me. I spin around, keeping a tight grip on the ax.

29

Before we locked the apartment and picked up our suitcases to leave for Grandma's, the last thing Mama did was phone Ruth. She sat on the bed in the room she shared with Papa, her back to the door. She was on the phone a long time, speaking in a low voice, though she mostly just listened, as usual. Occasionally, she would murmur brief remarks, which mainly seemed to affirm Ruth's words of wisdom.

"Yes, I really need this. I have to get away, try to rest a little. Get some distance from . . . well, from everything."

I waited in the front hall, impatient and eager to get going. Summer vacation had just started, and I was dying to see Grandma. And to get away from the claustrophobic bubble of life with my parents. I was looking forward to Grandma's vanilla rolls nearly as much as the calm in her apartment.

Mama and Papa had been fighting more than usual lately. They might start arguing because of a note that fell out of Papa's pants pocket when Mama was doing the laundry. Or because he came home late, and she demanded to know where he'd been. Papa never answered her questions or apologized, just tossed out some sarcastic remark. That would really set Mama off, and soon accusations would be flying. She would spew the names of various women, and each time they fought, a new name would be added to the list. Papa's response, however, never varied. *Cunt.*

And within minutes, Mama would surrender in defeat. I could never understand why her anger would disappear at that moment. Couldn't figure out why she would capitulate like that. But that's what happened. My mother devoted her days to helping others, mostly women, stand on their own two feet and confront deceitful spouses, who were sometimes also abusive. People who knew my mother described her as strong, competent, and reliable. No one knew that, in her own home, she showed a completely different side of herself. No one knew but me, that is. And Ruth.

"Mama!"

I stepped forward and knocked impatiently on the door frame.

"Mama, aren't we going? Come on!"

We took the bus to the station in town. That was where we'd catch the regional train to Grandma's. Mama sat silently on the seat next to me, staring out the bus window at all the greenery. I tried talking about various topics, like my latest bike ride or a program I'd seen on TV, but I could tell she just wasn't interested, and soon I fell silent too.

At the station Mama looked up at the board listing arrival and departure times and frowned. She muttered something about delays, so we rolled our suitcases over to a bench and sat down to wait. We spent the rest of the afternoon sitting there. Our train was delayed three times, and each time, Mama stood up to voice her frustration before compliantly returning to the bench. I thought it was the same pattern as when she fought with my father, but I didn't say that out loud.

Finally, an announcement was made: all southbound trains were canceled for the rest of the evening due to a downed electrical line. We got our money for the tickets back and were offered reservations on one of the early departures the following morning. The bus ride home was even more silent, if that was possible. By the time Mama stuck her key in the lock and opened the door to our apartment, she'd hardly said a word to me. I wondered whether she really wanted to take me with her to see Grandma anyway. Maybe she would have preferred to go alone. That's what I was thinking as we stepped into the front hall. But I soon had other things to think about.

There were no lights on in the apartment, and at first, I thought Papa wasn't home. But then I heard a sound. Tense whispering and excited giggles. I looked at Mama standing next to me and saw her body stiffen. She'd heard it too.

"Hello?" she called out. "Is anyone there?"

Then Mama did something so unlike her that my throat closed up. Normally, she insisted that everything be nice and neat, but now she marched straight in without taking off her shoes. I knew something was wrong, terribly wrong. Her footsteps echoed off the parquet floor. The next second, something white fluttered at the other end of the apartment. A woman's naked body came rushing out of the living room, heading for the bathroom. I managed to glimpse a big rear end, shaped like a full moon, before it disappeared with the rest of the woman. The bathroom door slammed shut, and I heard it lock from the inside.

Mama squared her shoulders and paused for a moment. Then she continued to the living room and looked in. I was still standing on the doormat and couldn't see what Mama saw, but I heard what she said.

"You bastard!"

She took me over to Ruth's. We already had our suitcases packed, and she dragged them along as we stormed out of the apartment. Nobody followed us; nobody tried to call us back. Despite pulling both suitcases, Mama was practically running. I was tired from the bus rides, not to mention sitting in the train station all afternoon, so I had a hard time keeping up. Besides, I was hungry. I begged her to slow down several times, but she never did.

As soon as Ruth opened the door, Mama burst into tears. Ruth motioned for us to come in and didn't seem the least surprised by my mother's reaction. Maybe she'd been through this before, on occasions when I wasn't there. Ruth led us into the kitchen, pulled out a chair for Mama and then sat down too. I hesitantly looked around the apartment for something to occupy me, but I saw only books, crocheted tablecloths, and dried flowers. It occurred to me that Ruth was alone. Clearly no husband or children lived here. Just Ruth and two cats.

I played with the cats for a while, until they'd obviously had enough. Then I went back to the kitchen, where Mama and Ruth were emptying the dishwasher.

"But I still don't understand it," said Mama in despair. "How could he? How the hell could he?"

She handed some plates to her friend, who put them away in the cupboard. Ruth seemed a little stern, almost disapproving. She probably thought it was time for us to leave her alone. I suddenly felt completely exhausted. But it wasn't just my body that was tired, it was all of me. I was worn out, sick of being dragged around.

"Mama, I want to go home."

She didn't answer. Didn't even turn around. She just raised her hand and waved me away. As if she were swatting at an insect. Under normal circumstances, that would have been enough for me to give up and retreat, but I wasn't thinking the same way I always had before. Things looked different now. I stared at my mother's back. I was her child, and I was hungry and tired, but she didn't seem to care. She didn't care at all.

"I want to go home now!" I repeated, louder and more insistent.

She still didn't turn around. Merely glanced over her shoulder to let me know that we were going to stay awhile longer. And she kept on talking to Ruth. I don't know what it was, but at that moment, I felt something stab inside me, something that felt like a sharp spear. Before I knew it, I went over to Mama and yanked on her sweater.

"Right now!" I shouted.

Ruth pressed her lips together, in what was presumably an attempt to smile, with a faint, accusatory twitching at the corners of her mouth.

"Now, now, now!"

When Mama finally looked down at me, her face was stony. She pulled out of my grasp.

"Listen to me, Greta. We're staying here until I say it's time to go. Do you understand?"

Then she turned her back on me again, shutting me out. It was a familiar situation, but this time I had no intention of quietly complying. I was going to make my mother listen to me. I wasn't going to settle for anything less than her full attention. The first time the words slipped out, they were so quiet I hardly heard them myself. When I said them again, I made a great effort to enunciate each word, feeling them rise up from my stomach and spill, full force, out of my mouth.

"You cunt!"

Everything stopped. Even time seemed to stand still. The words seemed to linger in the room, hovering over us for a moment. Only afterward did they seem real. Mama and Ruth stopped talking so abruptly that it was like someone had flipped a switch. As if in slow motion, Mama spun around to look at me. I saw her hand reach out, saw it come whistling through the air. And even before it struck my cheek, my face burned like a thousand fires.

All three of us stared at each other. None of us said a word. Ruth's hand fluttered up to her mouth. Finally, Mama cracked, falling to her knees in front of me and wrapping me in her arms. It probably took no more than a few seconds, but it felt like an eternity before she made an effort to bridge the distance between us. The words poured out of her so quickly that I felt dizzy just listening to them.

"Greta, sweetie, I didn't mean to . . . I just turned around and saw . . . You have to understand I didn't mean to!"

She kept on talking without giving me a chance to reply or react. Of course she hadn't meant to hit me; she was just upset and she turned around and saw me standing there, in the path of her hand. An unfortunate misunderstanding, that was all. After a while, she calmed down. Then a different look appeared in her eyes, and a different tone entered her voice.

"But I think it would be best if we didn't mention this to anyone."

Anyone. I knew at once who Mama meant. Papa. I wasn't supposed to tell him. Not him. All of a sudden, she was anxious for me to say something, to show that I'd understood. So I promised. Promised not to reveal what had happened that day in Ruth's kitchen. Not to anyone. Mama relaxed a little. Then she let go of me and stood up. And again turned away.

At that moment, my father's fate was sealed. He had three months to live.

30

The girl stops in her tracks. Wide eyed, she looks from me to the ax. But only for a second. Then her gaze shifts, and she begins looking around, as if searching for something. Or checking to see if something is still there. I watch as she studies the ground nearby.

Only now do I discover that the little wooden cross at my feet isn't the only one of its kind. At the edge of the clearing there are several more crosses, all of them made from sticks. And in front of each of them the earth and moss have been dug up and then put back in place. I'm in a forest cemetery.

The girl seems satisfied with her inspection, because a look of relief appears on her face.

"You haven't disturbed them."

"The graves?" I say. "Why would I disturb them?"

She gives me a long look without answering the question. I think I see shame in her expression. Then it changes again.

"So what are you doing here?"

She sounds like a landowner confronting a trespasser on her property.

"I'm looking for a cat," I tell her. "What are you doing here?"

The girl shrugs, refusing to look me in the eye. Her long, dull black hair flutters in the breeze. On both sides of the part in her hair, the roots are blond, and in the dawn light I can see a lot of split ends. I can't help thinking that she could use a good haircut. Some new clothes. And maybe a little mascara and lip gloss too. Then I remember my own sloppy attire, the way I've carelessly pinned up my hair and neglected to wash my face. Without my armor, I feel naked, vulnerable, exposed. From somewhere, the phrase *The best defense is a good offense* appears in my mind.

"Is this your creation? What exactly have you buried here?"

The girl gives me another of those long looks. As if she's assessing me. I assume I'll be found wanting and don't expect her to answer. But this time, she does.

"I'm sure you know."

Then she steps past me. I blink my eyes and slowly turn around. Mutely, I watch as my young namesake crouches down in front of the grave and carefully straightens the cross, getting it to stand more erect. Her words are ringing in my ears. Suddenly, everything falls into place. The girl and her scary friends. The knife with the bloodstained blade I found out on the island. The mutilated creature that lay next to it.

"The squirrel," I gasp. "Which one belongs to the squirrel? Or did you leave it on the island?"

The girl is still leaning forward with her back to me, but over her shoulder, I see her hand shaking as she touches the cross.

"No," she mumbles. "I didn't leave it there."

She gets up and stands there with her eyes fixed on the grave. Without saying a word, her whole body is telling me *here*. So that poor squirrel is here, in the ground, right in front of us. I swallow hard, allowing my eyes to sweep over the pitiful little row of crosses. The squirrel's grave is the second to last. A thought is taking shape in the back of my mind, but it vanishes when the girl starts talking.

"I made the crosses myself. And sometimes I come here to . . . look at them. But only if no one sees me. Mostly before dawn, like now. Nobody can know. It would be . . ."

She falls silent and I wait, giving her the time she needs. Nobody can know. I recognize that mantra. I know that *nobody* usually doesn't refer to strangers, but to the people closest to you. Family. Friends. Lovers.

"They're just animals. That's all. Just fur and guts. But I still can't help . . . I can't just leave them lying there afterward. I'd rather die."

She says the last words with great emphasis. Her voice quavers with suppressed emotion, and I notice that she's clenching her fists. Part of me wants to reach out and put my hand on her shoulder. But I don't.

"Why do you guys do that?" I ask instead. "What makes you torture and kill an innocent animal?"

Before the girl has a chance to reply, a light goes on in my head. I picture Alex's excited expression, see the pulsing of the blood vessel in his temple as he leans over me. I'm wearing nothing except the black silk tie. He has peeled the jacket and panties off me. That part of the role-playing is over. Now I'm lying on the double bed in the summer cabin, my wrists bound to the bedposts. Alex is caressing me, pinching my nipples. He lifts the tie from between my breasts and lets it slide through his fingers. Then he grasps the knot of the tie at my throat and slowly starts pulling. Tighter and tighter. Until my protests stop. Until my lungs are burning and I can no longer breathe. He looks into my eyes, and I know he must see the terror I'm feeling. Then he smiles. And pulls the tie a little tighter.

"Power," I say out loud, answering my own question. "It's all about power."

The girl turns around and looks at me with an impassive expression.

"What do you know about it? What do you know about anything?"

At first, I'm annoyed. But my anger quickly fades, and I notice how tired I am. Exhausted. The ax slips out of my hand and falls onto the moss at my feet with a muffled thud.

The girl is walking among the graves, straightening a cross if needed, using her hand to sweep away pine needles and fallen branches. She makes her way along the row of wooden crosses until she finally comes to the grave at the end, the one next to the squirrel's final resting place. She stands there, her back to me.

"How do you know where I live?"

She shrugs, then answers without turning around.

"It wasn't very hard to find out. It's easy to tell which houses are empty and which aren't. And you told us where the cabin was."

"What were you doing in my yard the other night? If you weren't there for my help, that is."

She doesn't bother to refute my assumption. Nor does she bother to explain. Silence settles over us. Slowly, my irritation returns.

"Say something! Tell me why you were there!"

She still doesn't answer. Angry now, I take two steps forward and grab the girl's arm, forcing her to turn around. At first, when I see her thin face crumple, I think she's crying. But I don't see any tears.

"I'm sorry," she says quietly. "Please forgive me."

I frown and shake my head, uncomprehending.

"What am I supposed to forgive? What have you done?"

She reaches out her hand and clumsily touches the top of the wooden cross in front of her. Then she turns to me again, giving me a long look. A rushing starts up in my ears. The ground sways under my feet. My temples are pounding. Out of the corner of my eye, I notice a fallen tree trunk. I stagger over to it and sink down, gripping the rough bark with both hands. The cross . . . The new grave . . .

What exactly have you buried here? I'm sure you know. Yes, I realize. I do know. And it makes me want to scream.

Smilla, sweet, lovely little Smilla. I'm so sorry.

31

No howl issues from my throat. No accusations, no laments. No sounds at all. Inside I'm fumbling to formulate appropriate remarks, but without success. Finally, a few words do slip from my lips.

"You asked me what I was doing here . . ."

The girl nods mutely. Makes no attempt to fill the silence, just waits for me to go on.

"And I told you I was looking for a cat."

Again she nods.

"Are you trying to tell me that . . . that you found the cat outside my cabin and took him?"

"Yes."

My mind seems both cloudy and clear at the same time.

"And then . . ."

Again, the girl refuses to complete my sentence. And this time I leave it unfinished. I see her hand reaching for the newest cross in the clearing, see her touching the top of the stick. Then my eyes shift to the ground where she's standing, and I picture the black-and-white body buried beneath her feet. I imagine what the cat must have endured before he ended up here. I want to shut out reality. I want to close my eyes, but I don't dare for fear of the sights that will confront me. Massacred bodies fluttering in the wind like bloody sails. No! I slap my face hard, forcing open my eyelids, which, in spite of everything, had fallen shut. I give the girl a defiant look. It can't be true.

"I don't believe you!"

For a moment, she doesn't move, then she silently reaches into her pants pocket and takes out something. She stretches out her hand toward me, her fingers curled around something. She takes my hand and places a thin pink object on my palm. Tirith's collar. My eyes blur; I feel like I'm flying forward even though I'm sitting still. As if I'm traveling through a hazy mist. Only when I'm certain that I'll be able to keep my voice steady do I speak again.

"His name was Tirith," I say. "He belonged to a four-year-old girl who loves him very much."

It seems important for this skinny teenager to know. That the animal she captured and deliberately placed in malicious hands had a name and an identity, that he belonged to someone who will be brokenhearted to know he's no longer alive. But maybe that sort of information is wasted here, I think as I look at the stony mask covering the girl's face. There are probably very different things that upset her.

"We were bound together by blood," I add. "My blood."

I don't explain about Tirith licking the wound in my hand. Let this girl think I'm crazy—if that's what she's thinking. I see her looking at the ground. The ax is still lying there, and it's closer to her than to me now. Quickly, she sticks out her leg and sets her foot on top of it. Then she picks it up and stuffs the handle under her belt.

"Listen to me," she says, crossing her arms. "Jorma was the one who said we had to get revenge somehow."

A joyless laugh escapes from my throat. I can hear for myself that it sounds like the laugh of a lunatic, but I can't stop it. Revenge? What she's saying is absurd.

"Is he nuts? Are all of you nuts? What have I ever done to you? Can you tell me that?"

She rolls her eyes, as if exhorting me not to be so stupid. Then she looks away, chewing on her lip.

"I thought Jorma would calm down after we found it again. No harm done, really. I tried to get him to forget about you, but he . . . When he gets in that kind of mood, it's impossible to know what . . . It's like there are no limits. Sometimes I even think he might . . ."

She stops and gives me a furtive glance, obviously uncomfortable. Like she's said too much.

"I thought if he got your cat, then maybe that would be enough."

I look at her, shaking my head in resignation.

"I don't understand. I really don't get what you're talking about."

She studies me skeptically, as if I've missed something important. Only after several seconds does it seem to dawn on her that I'm actually as clueless as I look. She takes a deep breath and then exhales noisily. She comes over to the fallen tree trunk and sits down next to me, keeping a small space between us. Even though it's August, she's wearing heavy leather shoes. She runs the tips over the ground, sketching some sort of abstract pattern.

"The boat," she says with a sigh. "It's about the boat, of course."

She looks at me to see if I'm following, but I shake my head. I still don't get it.

"Our boats," says the girl. "It's about our boats."

She's speaking with confidence, emphasizing the word *our*. I picture two boats in my mind. A skiff and a dirty white rowboat. I see the bloodstains on board, a red blob in one end. The girl sitting next to me is still talking. Maybe it's because I haven't eaten or slept properly for days. Maybe it's because of the pregnancy and its effect on both my body and soul. Or possibly it's because during the past twenty-four hours I've been desperately searching for two people who have disappeared without a trace. And instead of finding them, I've wandered farther into the fog, sinking deeper and deeper into the dunes.

That could be why I'm having a hard time seeing where the girl's explanation is heading. Or maybe it's some sort of defense mechanism, a way of resisting an idea that's brewing. It couldn't be . . . It can't be . . . I hear only fragments of what she's saying. *The last time. Left there. Disappeared. Found. The other side of the lake. Jorma. It was you. Revenge.*

From a distance, I hear a roaring sound. It gets so loud that I have to put my hands over my ears. But it doesn't stop. The world around me is shaking. It keeps going so long that I finally have to scream. Someone pulls my hands away and cautiously moves them down to my sides. Someone is holding their face close to mine and talking to me. I can't make out any of the words, but the voice is unexpectedly gentle. Finally, I realize it's the girl, Greta. She's intoning soothing words in my ear as she strokes my back. And she keeps at it until I calm down. Until the roaring has faded away, until the screams have left my throat shredded and my body exhausted. After that, we sit in silence for a while, next to each other. Then I turn to face her, and she turns to face me. And when our eyes meet, I start to speak.

By the time I'm done, after everything has poured out of me, the sun has reached the tops of the trees, and it's getting hot. I pull the anorak over my head and wipe the sweat from my brow. Greta pulls the handle of the ax from her belt and gives it back to me.

"I feel sorry for you," she says. "I wish there was something I could do."

"There is," I tell her. "Leave him. Do it now, this instant, before it's too late."

She gives me a wan smile.

"You're going to be a good mother."

Then I hear it. The ringing. It's in one of the anorak pockets. For what seems like the thousandth time in a row, I run my hands over the fabric, inside and out, yanking on the zippers and buttons to get to my phone. But this time, it feels different. Because now I know. *Actually, I knew all along.*

I press the phone to my ear. This time, what I hear is not just silence on the other end. This time I hear the confident, self-assured voice of a man.

"Hi, Greta. It's Alex. Did you miss me?"

32

That evening when we walked down to the boat. Me trailing behind the other two, my eyes fixed on Smilla's thin legs sticking out from under her pink cotton dress. Legs effervescent with life, containing so much energy that she had to skip, since ordinary walking wasn't enough. Something about those legs made me think of the movie that Alex had chosen for us to watch a few days earlier. It was the story of a pedophile, the violence of a child killer, a dark, depressing, merciless drama. When the camera finally zoomed in on the girl's pale, lifeless legs sticking out from under a bush, I could no longer hold back my sobs. I ran to the bathroom and threw up. Again.

Alex was still deeply engrossed in the film when I came back. He hardly glanced up when I sat down stiffly on the very edge of the sofa. I still hadn't told him about the baby. Part of me had thought it would become obvious, that he would notice I was constantly throwing up and put two and two together. But that didn't happen. He didn't find out until after we arrived in Marhem. And not until then was I prepared to tell him the news myself. That was only a few hours before Smilla arrived, a few hours before I would lie awake and make up my mind to keep the baby. And leave Alex.

The next morning, I told him, but he didn't take me seriously. I should have packed up and left right then, but something held me back. Was I trying to avoid making a scene in front of Smilla? Or was I simply surprised by Alex's reaction and needed time to pull myself together? Whatever the reason, I stayed that day. After dinner, I followed them down to the lake. Out on the dock, he turned to face me. The evening sun formed a bloodred halo around his head. He smiled.

"Nice to see you've changed your mind."

I was filled with a single, crystal-clear emotion. There was only one reply. As I recall, I didn't even have to steel myself before uttering the words.

"I haven't."

We got into the boat and went out to the island, where he disappeared without a trace. Went underground. I've been searching for several days now, trying to make contact, but without success. And all of a sudden Alex is back. His breathing in my ear sounds calm, self-satisfied. Apparently he has me right where he wants me. I press the phone harder against my ear so I won't drop it. I know he's waiting for me to say something, but I can't manage a single word.

"Clearly speechless from longing," he says at last. "Are you still in Marhem?"

I murmur affirmatively. I'm about to ask him where he is, but then I realize there's something I have to find out first.

"How is Smilla? She's not hurt, is she? You didn't . . ."

I can't finish the sentence. Fear and suspicion have plagued me ever since they disappeared. Fear of the unimaginable, the unspeakable. Even though there's no real reason for such anxiety. At least not based on the little I've seen of their interaction. Yet I've feared that Alex might hurt Smilla. That, for lack of other targets, he might vent his frustration on her, act out his inclinations on her. I can't bring myself to voice these concerns out loud. I can hardly bear even to think them. But that's the reason I stayed here in Marhem after they disappeared. Because I feel a weight on my shoulders, a burden that won't ease until I know that Smilla is safe. That nothing bad has happened to her.

I think about the elderly man in the brown house, who said he'd seen Alex and Smilla. I remember the words he used to describe Alex. *Angry. Or terrified. Hard to tell which it was.* Even though I didn't know how seriously to take the man's statement, it was his words that finally made me go to the police. For Smilla's sake. I've never seen Alex afraid, can't even imagine him being terrified. But I'm familiar with his inner fury, and I know all too well the kinds of things he does when driven by rage.

Alex takes the phone from his ear and speaks to someone nearby. "You're fine, right? Can you say that you're fine?" In the background, I hear Smilla's voice reply. With childish surprise, she repeats the words. "I'm fine."

I close my eyes, and the image of the girl's bare legs under the shrubbery melts away, leaving me finally in peace.

"Who are you talking to, Papa?"

Smilla is only four, but I can clearly hear a certain wariness in her voice. As I listen to Alex's explanation, something about an old childhood friend, the guilt returns. Guilt over my role in this girl's life, my intrusion into her world. I picture her. Her defiant little face when we pulled up to the island, and Alex trying to persuade me to go ashore with them. The look in her eyes when he said, with an irony she must have missed entirely, that this was a "family outing, sweetheart." She wanted her father all to herself. Not to share him with some strange woman.

I glance over my shoulder and see that the young, black-clad Greta has left the clearing. I'm alone once again, in the middle of the woods. In a primitive cemetery for animals, with an ax as my sole companion. On the other end, Smilla sounds unwilling to leave her father in peace, now that she knows he's talking to someone on the phone. "Papa is just going to talk a little while longer. You can go and use Papa's tablet if you want. Why don't you play that game you like so much? Yeah, the one with the girl you can dress up in different clothes."

Finally I hear a clicking sound, probably a door being closed, and there's silence in the background. No more Smilla listening nearby, jealously guarding her father. I touch the ax, take a deep breath.

"So tell me what happened that night on the island," I say. "Tell me."

And he does. Smilla was starting to get tired of the expedition when they came upon some sort of campsite on the other side of the island. A boat was tied up there, with what looked like bloodstains on the bottom. Smilla refused to get in, so he had to lift her on board. He explained that they were going to play a game and surprise me, that she would have to be very quiet and not yell or fuss. Then he rowed away from the island.

I shiver, in spite of the heat. I picture the white rowboat. I hear Jorma's hostile voice echoing in my head. *You haven't taken something that belongs to us, have you?* Then his voice changes. It's no longer Jorma I hear but the young Greta. *I thought he'd calm down when we found it again. No harm done, really.*

"Then what?"

"Well, then . . ."

Then they walked through the woods, heading toward the traffic sounds from the highway. And when they finally got there, they were lucky enough that one of the city buses happened past only fifteen minutes later. It was amazing timing, actually. Smilla slept most of the way home. He splurged on a taxi from the bus station.

And that was it. There was nothing more to add.

I run my trembling fingers over the anorak that I'd draped over the fallen tree trunk. Home. They're back home. They've been there ever since that night. While the abyss opened up beneath my feet, threatening to swallow me whole, Alex and Smilla were safe and sound.

He's been playing me the whole time. My head wags slowly from side to side. I knew it. Somehow I knew. But knowing something is not the same as understanding it.

"How could you do this?" I ask faintly.

His reply is like the crack of a whip.

"You really don't know?"

Mutely, I shake my head. Even though Alex can't see me, he seems to guess my response.

"I wanted to see how you'd react. If you'd leave right away. Or if you'd stay there and wait, try looking for us."

The tree trunk is hard and rough underneath me. I'm shaking all over. My hand is shaking so much I have to press the phone even harder against my ear or I might drop it.

My phone. The one I found in Alex's bed after they disappeared. Did it end up there by mistake, or did Alex deliberately put it there when he made the bed? When he decided to disappear with Smilla and make it impossible for me to reach him? Can that really be true?

"You turned your phone off," I manage to say.

"Not much of a challenge if you could have called me. Right?"

A roaring starts up inside me. Was that why he finally started calling me, but without saying anything? To heighten the tension, to increase the "challenge"? I ask him about the repeated calls, the silence on the other end, but Alex refuses to take credit for them. He steadfastly maintains that he hasn't called. When I persist, he gets annoyed.

"Who the fuck cares? It's not important. The important thing is that you didn't run off. You stayed, and that means you passed the test."

A whirling dizziness sweeps through my body, making my legs go limp. I've never fainted, but from what I understand, this is what it feels like before it happens. This chaos both inside and out, this darkness slowly sucking me in. Is that really what all this has been? A game? A test?

"Don't you understand it was for your own good? All those stupid things you said . . . I wanted to give you a chance to come to your senses. It's as simple as that. Make you realize that you can't live without me."

In my mind, I picture the black silk tie. I see Alex's hands pulling the knot tighter and tighter around my neck, while I, with my hands bound, arch my back in an attempt to get away. My eyes glaze over, my lungs are about to burst. I'm convinced that he's actually planning to strangle me. For real. Then, at the last instant, he lets me go. Lets me breathe again. *Realize that you can't live without me.*

Everything falls away, leaving behind only the truth, as hard and uncomfortable as the tree I'm sitting on. By subjecting me to this ordeal, Alex has purposely yanked away the already-rickety foundation on which my life rests. *It was for your own good.* The morning breeze sweeps through the trees, stroking its icy hand across my throat. Of everything he's put me through, this is the worst assault of all.

Somehow, I get up from the tree trunk and pick up the ax, but I leave the anorak where it is. Everything shimmers before my eyes as I walk back through the woods, not looking more than a couple of feet ahead. Branches scratch at my face, but the pain seems to be coming from somewhere far away, as if it's not part of me.

"And the child?" I hear myself ask.

"What child?"

"The baby that I'm . . ."

"There is no baby. You know that, Greta."

His words are charged with meaning. What he's saying, what he expects, is that it will just be the two of us. Until the next time he decides to play with my life. Because it will happen again, there's no doubt about that. Maybe he'll use the tie again, or maybe it will be something totally different. The only thing I know for sure is that he'll go one step further next time. And then one more step. He won't let go until I give up. Maybe not even then.

Alex is talking, listing all the clothes and toys they left behind in the cabin. Things that need to be reclaimed. And he's sure I realize that he can't possibly get away right now, so he wants me to pack up as many of his belongings as possible and bring them back in the car. He'll come over to my apartment as soon as he—

"No," I say.

"No?"

"No."

I'm thinking about the well, the one I pictured the other night when I was staring down at Lake Malice's dark waters. *If it really existed, I could have pushed you into it. That's what these days have taught me. That if I'd had the chance, I could have done it.* A person either gives up, or she fights back. And I am my mother's daughter. God help me, but I am. I know that now.

"I'm leaving you, Alex. I've made up my mind, and I'm more sure about this than I've ever been about anything else in my life. If you ever come near me again, I swear I'll kill you."

He doesn't say a word. Almost thirty seconds pass before he speaks.

"Like you killed your father?"

"Exactly."

I hear a hint of something in his voice. A slight quaver.

"Would you really do that?"

I let the silence speak for me. Let it be my only reply. Then I end the call. I hold the phone in one hand, the ax in the other. I plow my way between the tree trunks. Apparently, Alex has understood nothing about who I am. Absolutely nothing.

33

I rage my way through the woods. There's no other way to describe my progress. Dry branches jab at me, scratching my cheeks and forehead. Something warm is spilling from one eyebrow. My vision gets murkier instead of clearer; the shimmering before my eyes gets worse. When I finally emerge from the trees and come back out on the forest road, my whole body seems to be swaying, like I'm in the middle of an enormous, stormy ocean.

My legs carry me forward, and I let them take me, without knowing whether I'm heading in the right direction. And besides, what is the right direction? Something is coming toward me on the road. Something or someone. My hands tense painfully, and even though I can't really see the objects I'm holding, I know they're there—both are like extensions of my own body. The cell phone and the ax. At this moment, I've become one with them, clutching them tightly, vowing not to let them go, no matter what happens.

The beast coming toward me is dark and hairy. It moves quickly, agilely. I stop, thinking that it might not be real. To see something that doesn't exist, or not to be able to take in what actually does exist—maybe those are two sides of the same coin. Like what happened with Papa, that which escapes me. Is my memory failing? Why am I unable to correctly interpret what I see? The beast is close now, it comes right up to me, and I feel something soft and cold against the back of my hand. A dog's muzzle. Reality seizes hold, the veil is pulled aside, and suddenly I see clearly. Not looking outward, but inward. It's not a matter of a faulty memory or distorted experiences. What I'm missing is the will to acknowledge what happened to Papa. Who and what it has made me.

"I'm sorry," I whisper, and my eyes fill with tears.

I seem to see that the dog has taken a step back and is now licking his nose. Then he gives a loud bark, not sounding angry, but confused. Appealing to the person who comes walking up behind him.

"Hello again," says the man from the brown house.

Alex's explanation for how he and Smilla left the island and made their way through the woods echoes in my mind. I turn to look from the shaggy creature at my feet to the elderly man. I stare at him.

"You must have seen them when you were out walking your dog," I mutter, slurring my words. "You really did see them."

Something about my appearance seems to startle him. Then he calls the dog. A wave of nausea sweeps through me, followed by a strong pang in my abdomen. As if someone were sticking a knife into my guts. The pain makes me double over. I hear the man's voice, sounding both concerned and suspicious. Before I can answer, the stabbing pain comes again, and I almost fall to my knees. A thought races through my mind. *The baby.* I can't lose the baby. Not that too.

I force myself to straighten up and start forward. But the man is in the way. His features are hazy, his expression unreadable, but his voice now sounds very worried. Something lands on my shoulder, squeezing tight. Is that his hand? Is he trying to stop me? Trying to keep me here? Panic creeps over me, giving me renewed strength. Making me suddenly furious. Loud screams ring out across the road, spreading to the nearby woods. My throat is stinging, burning, and I realize the person screaming is me. Then it's there again, the hand, wanting to hold me in place. I lurch back to pull free as I raise my ax.

The wind subsides, the world stands still, and the only sound is the dog's pitiful yelping. The man steps aside. No, he doesn't step aside, he turns on his heel and leaves. He may even be running. Fleeing. Only when both he and his dog are gone do I realize that the man held out his hand not in a show of force but in self-defense. It wasn't intended to hold me there. It was to keep me away.

Somehow, I make it back to the cabin. Along the way my condition gets worse. The cramps in my stomach have faded, but now the pain has settled in the small of my back. Tugging and aching, with occasional stabs of pain. The pressure in my chest is so bad I can hardly breathe. I stagger over to the parked car outside the cabin and lean against it. The car isn't locked, so I open the door and fall into the driver's seat. My head feels like it's on fire. The shimmering before my eyes has changed to searing flashes of light. In this condition, I won't be able to drive more than a hundred feet. I'll end up in a ditch. Or crash into the mountainside.

What I need to do is make my way over to the highway and catch one of the buses that goes through Marhem. Just like Alex and Smilla did. I rub my forehead. I still can't really take it in. Slowly, I turn to look at the cabin. In my mind, I take an inventory of the suitcases, clothes, and toiletries inside. Everything that belongs to me, everything I'd need to take with me. Just thinking about it requires an enormous effort. Right now, I'm so exhausted that I can't even imagine getting out of this car. I have no energy. Another wave of vertigo swirls through, churning inside me, making the world twist and lose shape. I'll never manage it.

My belongings will have to stay here. There's no other option. But the cat. I should at least go get Tirith and bring him with me when I . . . The image of a little cross made from sticks cruelly interrupts my thoughts. A slender pink collar. Again I feel the impact of the black-clad girl's confession. I remember that Tirith isn't waiting for me in the cabin. That he's never coming back. That someone will have to tell Smilla. Smilla, who smells of apples and vanilla, who loves princesses and Barbie dolls. Smilla, who adores her father.

My face falls onto the steering wheel, pressing on the horn, which emits a single beep. There is something infinitely melancholy about that one-note sound. Both a sender and a receiver are required for a sound to have any meaning, but I'm the only one present to hear it. Out of context, the sound loses all meaning, becomes pointless. Just like me, just like my life so far.

My thoughts return to that last evening, to the sight of Smilla and Alex holding hands on their way to the dock. The jealousy and longing I felt at that moment are still with me. Could that be me in a few years? Holding a warm hand in mine, an eagerly chattering little person at my side? Or am I kidding myself? Am I allowing myself to be blinded by this new-old longing for closeness? The inheritance I carry. The inheritance my child will carry. Would that cloud everything? Would that destroy everything? *Oh, Mama, tell me whether it was worth it. Would you make the same choice again?*

At that instant, she calls me. I stare at my phone, which I'd tossed on the passenger seat next to me along with the ax. Mama? *Mama!* The last time we talked, I hung up on her. I haven't taken her calls for close to two days now. Haven't really talked to her in over twenty years. Not really. My temples are pounding. Everything I'd hoped for with Alex, everything I didn't get. I pick up the shiny little phone and answer without thinking.

"I don't want to be alone anymore."

34

I'm still in Marhem, still in the cabin. I'm lying in bed with my clothes on and the covers pulled up to my chin. In fact, I've pulled the duvet from the other side of the bed on top of me. From his side. The man who will never again lie next to me. *If you ever come near me again, I swear I'll kill you.* I'm shivering and my teeth are chattering, but I nod emphatically. I really do mean it. It could happen. I have it in me. For all these years, I've fended off that thought, the one lurking in the shadows. I've tried to convince myself I'm not like that. But to no avail. Now I know.

In spite of the double layer of blankets, my body is shaking with cold. A throbbing headache is making the daylight hurt my eyes. I should get up and pull down the blinds, but I can't muster the energy. *Mama,* I think, *hurry up.* She reacted with such calm when I fell apart on the phone. She asked me where I was. After I'd explained and given her clear directions, she said:

"Stay there. I'll come and get you."

"No, you won't. I waited so long, but you . . . you never came."

Thoughts and memories blended together in my agitated state. I saw myself sitting on the floor in my room, saw the uniformed officers come and go, saw Ruth come and go. And I saw the door to what had been Mama and Papa's bedroom. The door that remained closed for so long.

Mama was silent a second longer than necessary. Then there was something different about her voice. As if the outer layers had been peeled away.

"This time I'm coming. Right now. I promise."

And I knew she meant what she said. Taking action is my mother's forte. There has never been any doubt about that.

My eyelids flutter, and I realize I must have dozed off for a while. My joints ache, and my skin feels hot. I'm still in Marhem, alone, sick, and miserable. Tirith is dead. The search for Alex and Smilla is over. There's no reason for me to stay awake.

Filled with longing, I reach for the release that sleep brings. Allow myself to be swept away once more. I slip into a hazy space, drifting in and out of restless slumber. I dream that I gave my mother the wrong directions, and she's driving around and around without ever arriving, without ever finding me.

A knock on the front door wakes me. At first I think it's part of my dream, but then I realize it's real. I'm suddenly wide awake. Mama! She's here. Everything's going to be fine.

I'm still weak, but at least my body obeys when I force myself to get out of bed and head toward the front hall. I have no choice. Mama doesn't have a key, and in spite of my miserable condition, I was very careful about locking the door when I came in. I remember having a sense of some approaching threat. As I shuffle to the door, I'm frowning. What sort of threat did I imagine? From where? From whom? I can't recall now. *It escapes me.*

I'm at the front door. I reach for the lock. I picture the person standing outside. My hands are shaking. Why? Why am I shaking?

Because I'm sick, because I have a fever. Why else? I turn the lock and cautiously open the door.

"Mama?"

But it's not her. It's . . . I can hardly believe my eyes. It's my psychologist. The blond. The woman whose office I left years ago. The woman whose ominous words have been ringing in my ears these past few days. She's changed her hairstyle, and she's wearing different clothes, but I recognize her instantly. And I realize that I must be dreaming. This woman can't be standing here, on the steps to Alex's cabin. Not for real. The fact that she's holding an oar makes the whole thing even more absurd and dreamlike.

In a daze, I think there must be a reason for her to seek me out. She must have a message for me. Suddenly, I'm afraid I'll wake up before the dream version of the psychologist has time to tell me what she needs to say.

"You were right," I mumble. "Everything you said was right. But what now? What am I supposed to do now?"

She stares at me for a long time, opening her blue eyes wide and then narrowing them again.

"So it's you? It's you."

Then she raises the oar. *Maybe this isn't a dream,* I think. Maybe I'm delirious.

Then the psychologist emits a scream, shrill and piercing. Hysterical. I flinch. Because I know that voice, that scream. In a sudden moment of clarity, I'm carried back to the night we arrived in Marhem. The car outside. The one who stayed and the one who left. Smilla and the woman with the scream. Smilla and her mother. Smilla and Alex's wife.

I take a step back as something dark whistles through the air. It strikes my shoulder and the side of my head. I fall against the wall and throw out my hand, but in vain. I feel my body tumble to the floor. Then everything goes black.

35

It begins and ends with Mother. To understand me and my story, you first have to understand that. In the beginning, Mother was my everything, and I was hers. I was the light of her life, that's what she always said. Her voice was as soft as a caress on my face. She used to hold me in her arms, pressing me close to her warm flesh, making me understand that with her I would always be safe. A faint lavender scent rose from her skin when she stroked my hair. She got up with me in the morning and made breakfast, she was there when I came home from school, she tucked me in at night. Every day, every night. She never let work, or her women friends, or any other distractions take her away from my side. I can't remember a single instance when she wasn't there when I needed her. Everything she did was for me. Never in my life has anyone loved me like she did.

When the hospital called to say she'd been in a car accident, I was home alone with Smilla. Alex had gone to Marhem on his own to finish a big project. At least, that's what he told me.

"It's serious," said the nurse who called.

At that moment, a chasm opened up under my feet, another inside my chest. Those first years after I'd moved away from home and left Mother's safe *nest, I was a lost wanderer. I discovered that the world was an unpleasant and frightening place. I trained to be a psychologist, thinking that would help me to figure out why I felt like a cat adored in the summertime and then abandoned in the fall. But it was only after Smilla was born that the pieces fell back into place. I had a mission. Motherhood became my calling. And Mother became more than my safe haven. She became my role model, my guiding light.*

I gripped the phone, afraid to ask.

"How serious?"

"Come as soon as you can."

Smilla didn't want to go anywhere without Tirith and her toys, so I got out the cat carrier and our biggest suitcase and let her pack whatever she liked. The August evening slipped into night, closing its darkening walls around us as we headed for Marhem. I drove much too fast the whole way. I could hardly see because of the tears streaming down my face. Mother's footprints were about to be washed from the surface of the earth. Her example, which I had unsuccessfully tried to emulate, was about to fade. Who would I be without her? How would I be able to go on or bear what had become of my life?

The car parked in front of the cabin belonged to another woman. I realized that at once. Though I'd previously looked the other way, I couldn't do it anymore. I hadn't warned Alex of our arrival. I didn't call his cell phone until we were already standing in the road outside. Maybe I subconsciously wanted to take him by surprise. When he came out, I screamed at the top of my lungs. Screamed as if I was on the verge of losing my mind. Or as if that had already happened. That's what Alex would say, of course. It wasn't like me to behave that way. Not at all like the wife he had molded. The one who knows to yield, accept, look the other way. I don't remember what I screamed; maybe there were no real words or phrases. Maybe it was just one long primal scream, emanating from my fear that Mother was about to be taken from me. The other woman—you? You really weren't important. Not then.

The hatred crept in later, at the hospital. For two days and two nights, I kept watch at Mother's bedside, holding her hand, bargaining with the higher powers. If only she was allowed to live, I would . . . what? I had nothing to offer in return. I wondered what Mother would want me to do, what sacrifice she would have found appropriate. But the only thing I could think of was Smilla. The only thing that meant anything, that Mother would have considered meaningful, was that I look after my daughter. It was for Smilla's sake that I had to be willing to sacrifice everything. I thought back to that moment when we arrived in Marhem, when Smilla dashed out of the car and threw herself into Alex's arms. How she buried her face in his chest as he lifted her up. As if she was seeking shelter, as if he was the one who could offer her that. Alex and the woman waiting inside the cabin. Our cabin.

Hatred took over my body, filling me completely, seething and surging under my skin. I didn't know what to do with all the darkness and violence, didn't know where or toward whom to direct all those feelings. Then Mother died. There are moments—moments of terrible torment—when I think it wasn't from her injuries. It was the hatred that killed her. The hatred spreading through my body like a poison. It must have radiated out of me, must have seeped out of my skin as I held her hand in mine.

When I got home from the hospital, Smilla and Alex were there. We spoke very little to each other. I have no real memory of anything we said. Everything was blurry and clamorous, both inside me and all around, as if all boundaries were about to dissolve. I stayed in the bedroom, with the blinds down. Mother had left me. She had never taught me how to cope with a life where she no longer existed. Day and night, light and darkness, everything flowed together. I simply lay there, as if anesthetized.

Alex left me alone. At some point, I dozed off and dreamed that he came in, bringing me a tray of sandwiches and tea, that he sat down on the edge of the bed and put his arms around me. Consoling me. But when I woke up, the room was empty.

When my vision cleared, I noticed an object on Alex's nightstand. His cell phone. For a long time, I lay there, motionless, staring at it. Then I sat up and reached out my hand. I searched through the list of recent calls, found what I assumed had to be your name and number. And I called you. When you picked up, I ended the call. I did that several times. Secretly, whenever Alex wouldn't notice, I called. I didn't say a word, just listened to your voice on the other end. I closed my eyes and pictured you in my mind, tried to figure out who you could be and what your intentions were. But then something unexpected happened. You started screaming, swearing at me. I put the phone back and fell asleep. When I woke up, I was alone in the bedroom, and Alex's phone was gone. That's when I decided I'd had enough. I got up, took off my bathrobe, and put on my clothes. Then I went into my daughter's room.

We were sitting on the floor of her bedroom when I felt his eyes on my back. My hand tensed slightly, but I kept stroking Smilla's hair. I didn't have to turn around to know he was there or what his expression would be.

He was leaning against the doorjamb with his arms crossed.

"So, have you pulled yourself together?" he said. "Can we go on now?"

I knew he wasn't talking about Mother. He'd never been particularly fond of her. So I slowly nodded.

"I've been through this before," I told him.

Because I had. I spoke quietly, compliantly. The way he wanted me to. But I didn't look him in the eye, and I kept my back turned. It might have seemed like a silent protest—if I'd been that kind of woman. I clenched my jaw. He came back. That's what I tried to tell myself. This time too. He left Marhem, and here he is. That must mean something. But I couldn't shake the feeling that something was about to come undone, fall apart.

Smilla was sitting on my lap holding the tablet. She was immersed in some sort of princess game. She was so focused on what she was doing that she didn't even notice Alex there. Otherwise, she probably would have jumped up to throw herself into his arms. I felt a pang of jealousy. You have to get through this, *I told myself,* for her sake. *You have to do everything for your daughter, that's your commitment. The only thing of importance.*

"Children," I said out loud. "When there are children in the picture, you have to carry on. Nothing else matters."

I don't know what made me suspicious. Was it a sudden movement behind me? Did Alex shift position as he stood there in the doorway? Was he sending out signals of restlessness or disapproval? Maybe it was simply his silence that finally made me turn around. Alex, who was never without a reply.

We looked at each other, and what I saw in his eyes made me carefully let go of Smilla and stand up. When there are children in the picture . . . *An icy cold washed over me. I took a couple of steps closer and leaned forward, entreating him.*

"Tell me it isn't true," I whispered. "Tell me she isn't pregnant."

For some reason, I noticed that Alex was holding his phone. I stared at it. A few minutes ago, before I felt his presence behind me in Smilla's room, I'd heard the door to the study open. Hadn't the door been shut for a long time? What had Alex been doing in there? Talking on the phone? Who was he talking to? The answer was obvious, but I refused to acknowledge it. Slowly, I turned my gaze back to the face belonging to the man I had once promised to love, in sickness and in health.

He was smiling at me. One of his eyelids started twitching. An outsider might interpret these tiny, rapid movements as nervousness. But I knew it was something else entirely. Excitement.

"I need to know," he said softly, "how far you're willing to go for my sake. For the sake of our family."

When I married Alex, I was forced to move far away from Mother. When Smilla arrived, I cut my hours to part-time. Gradually, I stopped working altogether. I didn't see any of my former colleagues; I made no new friends. And I never, ever challenged him anymore. I'd learned not to do that after several experiences during those first years with Alex had cost me dearly. My social life, my work, my independence—that's what I'd already given up. What did I have left? What remained? Nothing. Even my mother was no longer in my life. And yet Alex asked me that question, hinting there was more I could do. While he . . . once again . . . with some woman . . . And in Marhem, in our cabin.

I don't know how it happened, but suddenly I was heading for the hall and the front door. Alex followed. When I paused to get the car keys off the dresser, he grabbed my arm. He swung me around, pulling my body close to his. His chest pressed against me, his eyes locked on my lips. As if he were going to kiss me.

"Without me, you are nothing."

Those words . . . How many times had he flung them in my face? I'd lost count. I felt the same way I always did when he said that. The same, and yet somehow different.

I pulled away and ran out the door. I didn't ask permission. I didn't say where I was going or when I planned to come back. Even I didn't know. My mind had stopped thinking. Time ceased to exist. The car drove itself. Only when I saw the sign for the exit to Marhem did I realize that was where I'd been heading all along.

There was a car parked outside the cabin, the same one as before. Your car. I parked behind it, got out, and stood next to the arborvitae for a while. Over the course of only a few days, everything had been taken from me. Not just Mother, but also my family, my orderly life. Shivering, I stared at the log-cabin walls visible through the hedge, thinking that you were inside. The person who refused to allow me to have my little corner of the world in peace. The person who had broken into my life and without hesitation had shattered it completely. The feeling that something was about to come undone returned. Back in the car again, I called home. Smilla answered.

"Mama, where are you? When are you coming home?"

I could hear in her voice that she missed me. She needed me, longed for me. For her mother. What Smilla had been forced to endure over the past few days, everything I hadn't been able to protect her from . . . I needed to compensate for all that.

I don't know how or why. I only know that I suddenly felt as if I were standing several feet above the ground. As if I'd risen from the ruins and shaken off the dust, stronger than ever before. Much had been lost, but not everything. I was going to fight for what remained, fight for what I had left. For what was mine.

I told Smilla I loved her, that she was the light of my life. I explained that Mama had to take care of something, but when that was done, I'd come home. Then she and Papa and I would live happily ever after. Then I asked to speak to Alex. As soon as I heard his voice on the phone, I told him where I was.

"The answer to your question," I added, "is that I'm prepared to do whatever it takes, to go as far as necessary."

I listened to my own voice, heard myself speaking with a composure I didn't feel. Then I waited. It took a moment before Alex said anything. I heard a crackling and scraping, as if he were silently deliberating as he ran his fingertips over the phone.

"The cabin is insured," he said at last. "If anything should happen, if it should, for instance . . . burn down. Then we'd get a lot of money. That might be something to keep in mind."

My neck felt stiff as I turned my head to look back at the cabin. I was suddenly aware of it again, the chasm that my chest had become when Mother died. It opened once more, and hatred poured out. Finally, I knew where to direct that hatred. Toward whom.

"That project you went to Marhem to finish," I then said. "Maybe I can help you with it."

"Is that what you want?"

"If you do."

"You would do that for me?"

"For us."

I end the conversation and get out of the car again. I walk up to the cabin and try the door. It's locked. I look under the steps, but the key isn't there. There's no turning back. I can't lose my courage now. Without Alex and Smilla, I don't exist. Without them, I'm nothing, have nothing. My eyes are stinging. Maybe with tears. But I pull myself together. Crying is not what I want to do. What I really want is to break your neck.

I never thought I had it in me. Until now. No, I really didn't. But now . . . Nothing is the same. Not even me. Especially me. Who knows what I do or don't have in me? To kill someone. I didn't think I was capable of that. But maybe I was wrong. Behind the shed is an old oar. I go over and get it. Then I knock on the door.

36

When I come to, I'm lying stretched out on a hard surface. My head aches, but in a different way from before. The pain is much more intense and focused on one side, and my scalp feels tender.

I instinctively want to reach up to touch my head, but I can't. My hands are bound, lying on my chest. With a sharp yank, I try again. The motion sends a surge of pain into my shoulder, as if it's being slashed by dozens of sharp knives. It hurts so much I almost faint.

I hear a scraping noise nearby. A shadow is moving on the periphery of my vision, and I can make out a low murmuring sound. Gradually, images of what happened before the world went black return. The woman outside. Her scream. The oar in her hand.

Again I move my wrists, but this time more carefully. I can feel the rope tied around them. My vision is blurry, and I'm having a hard time moving or shifting position. With an enormous effort, resulting in more searing pain, I turn my head so I can see more of the room. Where am I? Soon I've connected the hard surface with the closest objects in my line of sight: the lower part of a sofa and the legs of a coffee table. We're still in the cabin. I'm lying on the rug in the living room. She must have dragged me in here when I passed out. The tenderness on my scalp makes me think she dragged me by my hair.

Hesitantly, I move my legs, not surprised to find that they too are tied. I close my eyes again, feel the pain throbbing in my head and shoulder. A lethargy bordering on surrender spreads through my body. Even if I wasn't bound, I probably couldn't move, much less get up and flee. There's nothing I can do. Nothing except wait and see what happens.

The sound of cupboards being opened and closed in the kitchen reaches my ears. A hissing noise, then the clinking of glass striking glass, and after that, the sound of liquid pouring. Firm footsteps approaching.

"Here," says a stern voice. "Drink this."

I force my eyes open, and at first I have a hard time focusing. Then I glimpse a glass held out to me. The hand holding the glass is thin and pale. The same hand that once closed around my wrist and held me back, forcing me to listen. *Next time you encounter an overwhelming or surprising situation, the pattern will repeat itself. Things are going to get worse for you. And you risk being knocked off balance. In the worst-case scenario, that sort of state of mind could have very unfortunate consequences. For you, or for those close to you.* My former psychologist. And Smilla's mother. They're the same person. The faceless wife, the woman in the wings who had never seemed more real to me than a cardboard figure. It's her. The whole time, it was her. It doesn't seem possible. It's crazy. But that's how it is.

Even if I'd wanted to take the glass, I couldn't. The woman grunts impatiently, as if it's my fault that I'm tied up. She sets the glass down, seems to realize that I'll need some help to drink. She grabs me under the arms and harshly pulls me into a sitting position. I scream from the pain in my shoulder, but it doesn't faze her.

She props me up against the sofa, poking at me until my body seems to achieve some semblance of balance. Like I'm a sack of potatoes. An inanimate object. Then she holds the glass to my lips.

"Come on, drink this."

My throat is parched from thirst, and I obey, opening my mouth and taking a big swig. I feel a burning in my throat and instantly realize my mistake. Why would she give me liquor? I reflexively turn my head away from the glass and spit in disgust, trying to get rid of every last drop.

"What . . . why . . . ?"

My tongue feels dry and swollen, and I can't control it. But the disjointed words I utter seem to set her off.

"I know all about you two. Alex told me. I even know about the baby. A baby. You're expecting his child. You must realize that's something I simply can't accept."

She leans closer, and I catch a whiff of shampoo. A sweet, floral scent. Like Smilla. She smells exactly like Smilla.

"All right. Now drink the rest."

Her words ricochet off the walls as she holds the glass out to me. I look her in the eyes. They're light blue, the pupils small and piercing. Were they like that back then? When she sat across from me in her armchair and patiently listened to my evasive accounts of what might be really bothering me? Every question I asked was countered with another question. She never told me a thing about herself. Now she's sitting in front of me again, the same woman, and yet she's infinitely different from the one I knew back then.

A baby. You're expecting his child. I simply can't accept that. She doesn't intend to get me drunk. She's planning something else. We stare at each other. The hatred radiating from her is so intense that it's almost palpable. Did she possess that hatred back then? Concealed beneath the calm façade?

"You are . . . ," I venture hoarsely. "You said . . ."

Recognition. Everything depends on recognition. In spite of my dazed condition, I realize that I somehow have to get her to remember me. To see me, not just as the woman with whom her husband has committed adultery, but as a former client. Someone she had a professional relationship with, even a certain responsibility for. If I can just make her realize who I am, she won't be able to hurt me. Or the child inside me. I take a breath, tense my vocal cords, and find my voice.

"Psychologist. You're a psychologist."

Her face remains impassive. She doesn't even blink.

"Don't you remember me? I was—"

"Shut up and drink."

And suddenly I understand that she already knows. She recognizes me, knows full well who I am. But it doesn't matter. It's just an unlucky coincidence and has no bearing on her plans.

I slump, feel one side of my body slide a bit toward the floor. I want nothing more than to erase from my memory everything Alex ever said and did, everything that was us. And I want to do it this minute. I have no patience to wait. I want to rip him from my skin like a stubborn Band-Aid, not caring whether it's painful or whether the adhesive takes a piece of me with it. *A piece of me* . . . I swallow hard. What he left inside my body—if it's allowed to grow and live—is what truly has the power to remind me of him for all eternity. And yet. Slowly, very slowly, I move my head from left to right. *No, I won't do it.*

Hard fingers grab my chin and force my lips open. Before I understand what's happening, the liquid in the glass starts pouring down my throat. I can't breathe and have to swallow in order to get air. My eyes fill with tears, from pain and panic. My thoughts are whirling. The life growing inside me—I can't let her harm it. I fling my head so hard my chin strikes the edge of the glass and knocks it out of her hand. Then everything happens all at once.

My maneuver sends the pain shooting through my shoulder again, metallic and hard. What's left in the glass runs down my chest, soaking through my T-shirt. The alcohol stings as it spreads across my skin. At the same time, a hand slams against my cheek with a resounding slap, making my already-abused head feel like it's going to explode.

"Okay," she says. "Then we'll have to do it the other way."

Again she grabs me and more or less throws me onto my back on the floor. My torso lands with a smack. Blazing spears of pain pierce my head and shoulder. My vision splinters into scores of shimmering prisms, then slowly darkens around the edges. Somehow I have to stay conscious. I can't faint. That's all I'm thinking about.

I sense that she's moving away from me, heading for the front door. And suddenly, another thought occurs to me. The ax. If she finds the ax, it's all over. I whimper. Somehow I need to get up and defend myself, fight for my life. But I can't bring myself to move. Can't even roll onto my side. *So let's get it over with,* I think.

She slams the front door behind her. I don't hear a key turn in the lock, but it doesn't matter. I'll never get up off this floor. Darkness is creeping in. I look up at the ceiling again and pass out.

37

Stomping footsteps. Someone muttering about gasoline. "I'm sure there was a can out in the shed." Then I hear Mama's voice. Surprised and wary at first, then worried and upset. Then it stops, abruptly, midsentence. Minutes pass. Again I lose track of time. Then my eyelids flutter open, and I glimpse a familiar outline. She's sitting some distance away from me, very still. *Mama! You found me, you came!* That's what I want to shout, but my voice refuses to obey. Somehow, I manage to move enough to draw my mother's attention. She gasps, leans forward. Her whole being emanates concern.

"Greta," she says. "I'm here now. Are you okay?"

Is she tied up too? Is that why she doesn't rush to my side? My lips form words, but nothing comes out.

"Please," my mother begs, turning her head. "Let me go to my daughter and see how she is."

"So she's your daughter?"

The voice drips with scorn. I wrench my gaze in the direction my mother is looking and see her. She's leaning against the wall, no more than a couple of feet from the chair where my mother is sitting. Long blond hair falls over her face in profile. A blue, flowered summer dress and a light cardigan. Ordinary, commonplace. She'd look like any other woman if not for the long black object in her hand. As soon as I realize what it is, my spirits, which had leaped at my mother's presence, sink again. She found the ax. The one I bought to defend myself. Now it's easy to see why Mama doesn't dare move without permission.

"Let me go to her."

The psychologist feverishly runs her hand through her hair. When her fingers get caught in a tangle, she yanks hard several times until she pulls free. Her movements are erratic, and she seems confused, uncertain. Not at all like when it was just the two of us.

"Why should I?"

When she came to the cabin, I was alone, as she'd expected. Mama's arrival must have caught her by surprise.

"Do you have children?" Mama asks without the slightest quaver in her voice. "If you do, I know you understand."

Silence for a moment. The psychologist seems to be deliberating with herself. Finally, she waves the ax in front of Mama's face.

"Okay, but remember—I've got this. If you try anything, I won't hesitate to use it."

The next second, Mama is kneeling at my side.

"Sweetheart. What have you gotten yourself into?"

Gently, she takes my face in her hands, moving her cool fingers over my cheeks and down to my throat. She can't help grimacing, and I think to myself that she must see it. The mark from Alex's tie. How should I answer her question? Then I remember the branches that scratched at my face in the woods, and the cut above my eyebrow, and the oar that slammed into the side of my head and shoulder. I think about the liquor that spilled over my chest, about the tenderness on my scalp, and my bound hands and feet. A three-day-old bruise is probably the least disturbing thing about my appearance right now. Mama leans close, as if to kiss my cheek. Instead, I hear her whisper in my ear.

"I didn't know she was here. She attacked me, took my purse and my phone, the minute I . . ."

Quick footsteps approach. Mama is yanked up. As she's led away, I hear her pleading, "From one mother to another. All those bruises and cuts . . . My daughter really needs me right now. And she has a high fever. She's burning up. At least let me give her some water."

The talk of water makes me painfully aware of my parched throat. My head feels like it's on fire. I need to get something to drink soon. I really do. But the psychologist's patience has apparently run out, along with her uncertainty about taking action. Brusquely, she shoves my mother back into the chair where she was sitting before.

"I don't have to do anything," she says coldly. "The only thing I need to do is finish this."

She leans over Mama to do something, but I can't tell what it is.

"You don't need to tie me up," Mama says quietly. "Even if I did manage to untie Greta, she's in no shape to go anywhere. And I'm not going to try to escape. I'm not leaving this cabin without my daughter."

The psychologist pauses for a moment. I can see from her back that she's hesitating. Then she shrugs and stops what she was doing.

"You shouldn't have come here," she mutters. "I don't intend to leave any witnesses."

Finish this. Witnesses. A shiver ripples through my body. Alarmed, I try to move. I feel the rope biting into my wrists.

"What exactly are you planning to do?"

Mama's question goes unanswered. There is a stiff quality to the psychologist's body language. She holds the ax tightly in both hands. My eyes are fixed on my mother's face. On her upper lip, where tiny beads of sweat have formed. For a long moment, no one speaks. Then Mama slowly stretches out her hand toward the ax.

"Give it to me," she says. "Give it to me so you don't do something you'll regret."

It's that tone of voice, controlled and authoritative, that I know so well. I feel a prickling under my skin when I hear it. *No, Mama, don't. Don't do it.*

"You don't want to do this," Mama continues coaxing. "Not really."

"Be quiet."

The psychologist steps to the side, blocking my view. I can't see my mother's face anymore. I can only hear her voice.

"I think that deep inside you're a smart and sensible woman. You're extremely angry right now. You know you can't harm Greta. You know it wouldn't be right."

Dread is swelling into a howl inside of me. A tiny muscle in the psychologist's jaw is pulsing. *Don't you see it, Mama? Don't you understand?*

"Shut up and sit still."

But Mama doesn't do as she's told. She gets up so that she's standing face-to-face with the woman, both of them the same height.

"Let me tell you about my daughter."

"I'm warning you."

"Because if you knew Greta the way I do, if you knew what she's like, you'd never be able to harm her."

Something in Mama's voice touches me, and the dread gives way to something new. But that lasts only a moment. Then the psychologist raises her voice. Her hand jabs out, and as she shoves Mama to the floor, she screams so loud it makes my ears ring.

"I do know. I know exactly what your daughter is. She's a whore and a murderer!"

She spins around, moving so fast that her blond hair whips through the air. She fixes her smoldering gaze on me. Lifts the ax. And lunges forward.

38

I must have closed my eyes, because for a moment the world went black. Then I hear a scream, and I open my eyes. A few feet away, Mama is lying on the floor, one arm stretched toward me. Standing between us, next to the coffee table, is the psychologist. Her arms go up and then come down. The ax plunges with terrible ferocity through the air and strikes its target, chopping it in two. The table protests with a loud creaking that is swiftly and mercilessly silenced when it splits in half after she's repeatedly hit it. Instinctively, I turn away to protect my face and the front of my body. With unseeing eyes, I stare under the sofa, listening to the butchering of the table going on behind my back. Something hard hits my hip, and a dry, lifeless tile comes flying and lands on my face, which is covered with cold sweat.

After what seems like an eternity, I no longer hear the sound of the ax whistling through the air or the wood shattering to pieces. For a few long moments, I don't dare turn around, afraid of what I'll find. But finally, I cautiously roll over to face the room. The object on my hip falls to the floor and rolls away. It's one of the table legs. The remains of the coffee table are scattered all over the living room, in pieces big and small.

Mama is still lying on the rug. She has her hands over her ears, and she's whimpering quietly. The officious expression and sensible tone of voice have vanished. Her controlled façade has cracked, the protective armor has been stripped away. Now she is simply herself. Simply my mother. The psychologist sinks to her knees in front of her and pulls my mother's hands away from her ears.

"Now it's your turn to listen as I tell you a little about your beloved daughter. Do you know that she seduced a married man, a family man? My husband, Smilla's father."

My mother peers over the woman's shoulder to look at me. Beneath the fear, I read the agonizing questions in her eyes as clearly as if she'd spoken them aloud. *So this is the woman who . . . ? It's her husband you've . . . ? And the child you're carrying . . . ?* I look away, as pain and exhaustion take over again.

The psychologist sits cross-legged on the rug, piling up pieces of the broken table. She moves mechanically. Her hair is tucked behind her ears, leaving her face visible and unobstructed. My vision is sharper now, and I see her clearly, noting the tense features, and the dark smudges under her eyes. *I see you. I mean, I really see you. I truly do. And I want you to know that.* Did he once say the same things to her? Was that how it started for her too?

"The part about your husband . . ."

Mama's voice is faint, wheezing. She leaves the sentence unfinished. Instead, she starts from a different angle.

"But murderer . . . I don't understand why you'd say that . . . What do you mean?"

The psychologist doesn't seem worried about having her back to Mama. And in spite of what just happened, the woman doesn't seem to have reconsidered her decision not to tie her up. I suddenly realize why.

She knows she's holding the trump card, that as soon as she replies, the final blow will be delivered, rendering my mother helpless.

"Several years ago, before all this happened, your daughter was one of my clients. She came only a few times, but she told me . . . Well, let me put it this way: I know about your dirty little secret. That your daughter pushed her father, your husband, out the window. That she killed him."

Silence falls like a lid over the room. For a long time, I can't bring myself to look at my mother. But finally I have to, of course. She's lying on her side, looking up at the ceiling, with her lips parted. I can't take my eyes off her face. It looks like it's been smashed to smithereens, and then somebody put the pieces back in all the wrong places. I haven't seen that expression in years. Not since that night. Then her gaze slides across the ceiling, down the wall, down to meet my own.

"You told her? I thought we promised each other never to tell anyone what happened."

For the first time in ages, I see something small and pitiful in her eyes. Something helpless.

"Mama. Please. I was eight years old."

Maybe I say it out loud, maybe I only think the words. I'm not sure, because of the pain and feverish chills. Mama's gaze clouds and turns inward. She slips away from me, inside herself.

"Yes, of course." At least that's what I think she murmurs. "Of course."

The psychologist keeps working, with great concentration, moving quickly. After a while, she turns to the magazine rack and pulls out a stack of newspapers. She tears them up with the same ferocity with which she attacked the coffee table. Then she places some of the torn pages under the piled-up pieces of wood, others on top. The ax is lying in her lap as she sits there cross-legged.

With a start, I realize what she's doing. She's building a fire.

A tiny swirl of nausea rises in my stomach. So that's her plan. To light a fire here on the floor. To dash out as soon as the flames take hold and blockade the front door. She probably already closed and locked all the windows while I was out cold.

I won't be able to get out once the fire starts. Even if I could stand up and stagger to the door, the woman wouldn't allow me to escape the flames. She's going to do everything she can to make sure I stay inside the cabin until it's totally engulfed. By that time, it will all be over, of course. How long does it take for a room to fill with smoke, for all the oxygen to be used up? No more than a few minutes.

I turn my head to the side, open my mouth, and let the vomit pour out. I feel like I'm falling, sinking. There's no hope of rescue.

If only my mother could escape. She really shouldn't have been here. She has nothing to do with any of this. Out of the corner of my eye, I see her slowly prop herself up on her elbow and move into a sitting position. Even though we're in the same room, her voice sounds far away, like it's coming from a great distance.

"I know exactly how you feel."

I'm not the one she's talking to. The psychologist stops and turns to look over her shoulder at my mother. Something flickers across her face. A tiny trace of hesitation. Then she goes back to what she was doing. She studies the tables and shelves, finds what she's looking for. A lighter. She gets up, grabs it, and comes back to the pile of wood on the floor.

"In most cases," my mother says, "I suppose people lie and try to hide their affairs. But not my husband. He enjoyed throwing them in my face, using them as a weapon when we argued. The simple truth is that he enjoyed hurting me."

Mama is staring straight ahead. Her hair is in disarray, and her blouse is wrinkled, but she pays no attention to her appearance. Her words sound naked, entirely earnest. The psychologist's hands are still moving, but am I right in thinking they've slowed down? Like she's waiting for something? Mama goes on, still not looking at either of us.

"During our years together, he cheated on me constantly. There were always new women. I often dreamed about taking revenge. About scratching someone's face to shreds. Grabbing some woman by her long hair and banging her skull against the ground. Destroying her. But later, I realized . . ."

The psychologist's hands are shaking now. She fumbles with the lighter, not making any real attempt to produce a flame. Her long hair is hanging in front of her face, hiding her eyes. Several seconds pass.

A muted voice says from under the blond mane: "What did you realize?"

"That I was pointing my revenge fantasies in the wrong direction. That those women had nothing to do with it. That he was the one who had chosen to ruin the life we shared. He was the one who was destroying our life."

I squeeze my eyes shut. Wanting and yet not wanting to listen. If Mama doesn't stop, if she tells everything . . . Emotions are turning me inside out, growing so strong that I'm about to throw up again.

The psychologist's thumb is moving up and down, flicking the lighter, but then letting it go out. She does this over and over.

"This is what he wants," she says at last, almost defiantly. "He told me to."

So Alex knows she's here, knows about her plan. Not only does he know, he's ordered it. He wants her to get rid of me. The room spins. I feel his hand on my cheek, the pat he gave me the morning when I told him I was going to leave. *No, you won't.* And I hear his voice on the phone when he finally called. *I wanted to give you a chance to come to your senses. It's as simple as that. Make you realize that you can't live without me.* Realize that I can't live without him. This was what he meant. Literally.

"I understand. And is he a good father? Will he be able to compensate for your absence while your daughter—Smilla is her name, right?—while Smilla is growing up?"

Mama's voice is almost unnaturally calm. The psychologist frowns. "What do you mean?"

Slowly, my mother scoots forward, closer to the other woman. Involuntarily, I clench my hands. The rope resists, chafing against my skin. *The ax, Mama, you have to take the ax away from her.* But my mother doesn't lunge forward. Her reason for moving across the floor seems to be so she can look the woman in the eye. Force her to look up from the lighter and meet her gaze.

"Murder or arson. Both are very serious crimes. You'll get a long prison sentence. Maybe life. I assume you've thought of that. And he has too. He must have taken that into consideration when he asked you to do this."

Silence again. For a long time.

I feel a burning sensation on my face, and when I look up, I discover that the psychologist is staring at me. Clutching the lighter, she points her finger. Those piercing blue eyes bore into me, but she addresses her words to my mother.

"You stood by and watched your daughter kill your husband. Then you protected her, let everyone think it was an accident."

Mama takes a deep breath, and I realize she is mustering her courage, trying to steady her voice.

"Is that what Greta told you? Is that what she said happened?"

The psychologist brushes back her hair and juts out her chin.

"No. Not in so many words. She didn't dare confess, when it came down to it."

She utters a joyless laugh.

"*It escapes me.* That's all she said. I remember it so well. She was obviously lying. Anyone would remember something like that."

Mama doesn't answer, just nods, as if to herself. Then she gets up from the floor, staggers the rest of the way over to the psychologist, and stands right next to her.

"That's not what happened. Not really."

She pauses for a moment, then kneels down again, leaning close to the woman. So close that they almost bump noses.

"I think you know what really happened. And why things had to turn out the way they did."

I close my eyes. Time stands still. Silence is all that exists. Mama's words hang ominously in the stifling air. Are they still looking at each other? If so, what do they see in each other's eyes? My tongue feels dry and swollen in my mouth. My shoulder and head are pounding, just like the excruciating pounding of my heart.

After a minute, I hear footsteps approaching, sense someone squatting down next to me. Cautious fingertips stroke my cheek, and when I open my eyes and look up, Mama's face is hovering above me. She smiles faintly.

"You poor thing," she says. "All these years. And now this."

Without hesitation, she leans down to untie the rope around my wrists. I expect the psychologist to stop her. I expect to see her come rushing over with the ax, yelling threats. But that doesn't happen. After Mama manages to pull off the rope binding my hands, she turns her attention to my ankles. As she tugs and pulls at the knots, I cast a surreptitious glance at the psychologist. She's sitting motionless on the rug, in front of the unlit pile of wood, her eyes locked on the lighter in her hand. After freeing me, Mama gets up with a muffled groan. Then she stands there, breathing hard for a moment before she again turns to the woman in the middle of the room.

"I'm going to the kitchen to get my daughter a glass of water. When I come back, I'll tell you a story if you like, a story about mothers and daughters and what can happen to deceitful husbands. But you'll have to put that down."

Then she goes out of the room, leaving me alone with the psychologist. I feel my body stiffen. But the other woman doesn't move. She doesn't even glance in my direction. She's just sitting there, holding the lighter between her thumb and index finger. I hear my mother moving around in the kitchen. I hear her turn the faucet on, then off. And then she's back, carrying a big glass of water in her hand. She pulls me up into a partially seated position, with one arm around my back, and helps me drink. The feeling of cool water running down my parched throat is so exquisite it makes me giddy, and for a moment I forget all else.

After I empty the glass, Mama sets it on the end table. Then she turns to the psychologist. I follow her gaze, see the other woman hesitate briefly before she tosses the lighter aside. Mama goes over and picks it up.

"The ax too," she says. "I can't talk with that thing in the room."

Without a word, the psychologist picks up the ax lying next to her on the floor. She stands up, weighing it in her hand. For a moment, it looks like she might actually comply, but then she changes her mind. The ax will stay. She makes do with lifting the nearest corner of the rug and sticking the ax underneath. Then she sits down in an armchair and wraps her arms around her torso without looking at either of us.

"Go ahead and tell your story," she says. "Then we'll see."

Mama takes a deep breath. She sinks down on the sofa behind me.

"Okay," she says after a long pause. "I'm going to tell you what really happened on a late September night long ago."

I can't see her face from where I'm sitting on the floor. I realize that's the way she wants it.

39

Unlike Greta, I remember every detail from that night. Like the fact that I was freezing, but didn't ask him to close the window. The cigarette in his hand, the reddish glow that flared every time he took a puff. I even remember how the cigarette paper disintegrated. And I remember what he said. Every single word.

What was left of the amber-colored liquid in his glass sloshed back and forth when he lashed out at me. It was his modus operandi, of course. The best defense and all that. That was his motto. Whatever I confronted him with, what I'd seen or heard or realized, was always handled the same way. He neither confessed nor denied. Nor did he apologize or beg forgiveness. Instead, he turned scornful and mocking, launching a counterattack and letting me know what a disgusting person I was. And even more disgusting as a woman. So repulsive that I made his dick shrivel up. Ugly enough to stop a clock. Finicky and complaining. A real cunt.

I used to think I was putting up a good fight. That I was strong. That he needed me even though he didn't realize it. I convinced myself I was the same person with him as I was at my job, with my friends, out in the world. Someone who refused to be provoked or humiliated. That worked relatively well. Until he knocked my legs out from under me once again. *Cunt.* I don't know why that particular term had such an effect on me. I only know that when he hurled it, I lost everything—my voice, my balance, my composure.

It was as if he'd torn off all my clothes to expose my nakedness. As if he'd pried my ribs apart and stuck in his fist and rummaged around until he found the scared little jellylike lump that was the real me. He held up that lump between us, forced me to look at it. Then he forced me to acknowledge what he already knew, what he'd claimed all along: that no matter how hard I tried to fool myself and the rest of the world into thinking that I was smart and special, deep inside I was nothing but a pitiful, colorless, trembling little lump. That's all.

Outwardly, I did everything in my power to maintain the façade. Not that I was afraid people would find out what he was really like, this man I'd married. No, I was afraid they'd discover me, that jellylike lump, underneath the competent, robust surface. Ruth was the only person who knew, who was allowed to see how fragile I was. I met her through my job. For a while, we worked in the same department, and when the agency reorganized, we stayed friends. By then, Ruth had become not only important but essential for me. With her steady and sensible nature, she was my lifeline. I trusted her implicitly.

But back to that night. Just when I thought the argument was over, as I was about to put on a sweater and go out for a walk in the neighborhood to calm down, something happened that would change everything.

"I know what you did to Greta. Hit your own child? How could you?" he said.

His voice was sharp, his words as cold as the air outside the window. We stared at each other in silence. Out of the corner of my eye, I remember noticing a patch of white in the doorway, but I couldn't tear my eyes off his face. Shame opened a chasm in the floor beneath my feet, sucking me downward. But I was forced to pull myself together. I had to.

"What did Greta say?"

He took another drag on his cigarette, lifted his chin to blow the smoke high into the air, and then laughed.

"Greta? She didn't say anything. It's sick how fucking loyal she is to you."

"But then how . . . ? Who . . . ?"

The world stood still, and at the same time seemed to be whirling so fast. He stared at me for a long time, one eyebrow raised.

"Well. Who do you think?"

"There's only one person who knew, and she would never . . ."

Ruth would never betray me like that. That's what I meant, even though I didn't finish the sentence. He shrugged, that sneering smile still on his face. Stubbed out his cigarette. Settled himself more comfortably, with both legs drawn up in the bay window. He downed the rest of his drink, not saying a word, waiting.

I thought about Ruth. The expression on her face when I tried to explain what I'd done in her kitchen, when she listened to my pleas. *Ruth, this has to stay between us, okay? You know what would happen if it got out at work. It would get blown out of proportion, turned into something that it's not. I would be the woman who hits her own child, and nobody would ever . . .*

It's true that things had seemed more strained than usual between us since that night. But no one at work had found out, I was sure of that. I would have noticed. Ruth hadn't said anything to them. So why would she have told him? My husband, of all people? Out of concern for Greta? Because she worried I might hit her again? No, Ruth knew me better than that.

"But why?" I managed to say. "Why would she tell you about that?"

Maybe at that point part of me was aware of the little figure off to the side who had started to move and was coming closer. If so, I didn't really register it. I was no longer receptive to any outside input. Everything was drowned out by the answer he gave, the insinuating tone of his voice.

"Oh, come on. Isn't it obvious?"

And suddenly it was. My mind created a frame around what had taken place at Ruth's apartment on that night. A frame that contracted and focused, zeroing in on details I had naively overlooked. The fact that when Ruth opened her door, there was already something different about the way she greeted me. The tense look on her face when I told her about the naked woman in my living room. And the way she immediately got up from the kitchen table, turned her back to me, and began emptying the dishwasher. She said maybe I should have thought about that earlier on. I asked what she meant.

"You have a very charismatic husband," she said. "You knew what you were getting into when you married him."

Maybe I should have paid more attention to what she said. It was so unlike Ruth. Maybe I should have had a stronger or different reaction. But at that moment, Greta came into the kitchen, wanting to go home. Everything was chaos inside me. Frustration, despair. And then she flung that word in my face, my own daughter. One thing led to another. My hand flew through the air, landing on my child's cheek. So fast. Everything happened so fast. Just as it did that night three months later.

I didn't simply walk over to him, I rushed at him. Holding my palms out in front of me. I slammed them against his chest and the side of his body as hard as I could. I saw the surprise in his eyes, how his face contorted as he plummeted through the open window. He'd never expected anything like that. I'd caught him off guard.

Suddenly, Greta was there, next to me. She reached out through the open window, but it was too late. He'd already been swallowed up by the dark. Maybe their eyes met one last time, father and daughter. Maybe they didn't.

Afterward, I spent a full night and day lying on the bed alone, with the door closed, cut off from my daughter. People spoke to me, but I had no words to offer in response. At first, all I had were screams and tears, which I'd kept so firmly at bay before. Later, when my body had emptied itself out, silence settled over me. It took twenty-four hours before I could muster enough strength to get out of bed. Twenty-four hours before I could make myself look into the eyes of my eight-year-old daughter. I took her in my arms, feeling how she huddled close as I whispered in her ear. I whispered that it was over now, that we would move on, stay together, and that she could count on me.

I said all that. But I didn't ask her for forgiveness. As soon as I went into her room and met her eye as she sat there on the floor, I knew it would be impossible. She would never forgive me.

Twenty-three years later, we never speak of what happened. And I don't need to ask what I took from her. Or what sort of person I became. For that, she has still not forgiven me.

40

Tears spill out from my closed eyes and run down my face, hot with fever. They refused to let me see Papa afterward. I'm not sure I would have wanted to see him, but it wasn't something they even considered. It was simply out of the question. That told me he must have been terribly battered. I imagined his crushed skull, cheekbones and nose smashed in so that nothing remained of his face but mangled flesh. It was too much to take, so I decided early on to think about it as little as possible. Preferably not at all. Instead, I created other images. The same way I created other explanations. *It escapes me.*

Mama's words have dispelled the fog. Exposed what I've worked to repress. Exposed the wedge that was driven between us that night, and the divide that has grown over the years. But her confession isn't the only thing overwhelming me. There's something else.

A hand reaches out from behind to rest on my shoulder. I want to touch it, but I can't. I blame the numbness in my limbs, but I'm not sure that's the whole explanation.

"I'm so sorry, Greta. For hitting you that time. And afterward . . . for shutting you out, leaving you alone so long. That was a terrible thing to do. Unforgivable. But I hope you'll be able to . . . I . . . I'm so sorry. I don't think I've ever said that properly."

Tears are still coursing down my face, slowly, quietly, as old, frozen emotions dissolve and ebb away. Tears of sorrow and anger, but also of shame. I missed my father, grieved for him so fiercely my whole body ached. And yet. Life after him, without him, was so much easier. Calmer. No moods, no nightly arguments. Mama was nicer. And happier. It was a relief. And I'm ashamed to admit it.

Mama's hand first squeezes, then caresses, my shoulder. She gets up and asks the psychologist where the bathroom is. When she comes back, she has refilled the water glass for me. In her other hand, she's holding a damp washcloth. She kneels down and gently cleans my face, wiping away the blood and tears. I look at her hands. *Those hands!* The hands that . . . I close my eyes and see two hands, palms out, shoot through the air and shove a man's body so hard that he falls. The same thing I saw when I fixed my eyes on the water of Lake Malice. Except the man I see now doesn't fall into a well, but out a window. And the hands I see aren't mine, but my mother's.

"Mostly superficial cuts," she says. "But you have a fever. And you're going to have big bruises here, on the side of your neck and on your shoulder. Does it hurt?"

I flinch and grimace when she touches the place where the oar struck me.

"You did the right thing. Absolutely the right thing."

The voice from the other side of the room sounds harsh. Mama's hands stop moving. The psychologist has turned to stare out the row of windows facing the deck. I signal that I need to lie down again, and my mother helps me. Then she goes back to washing my face, not stopping until I cautiously push her hand away. Again, she goes to the kitchen, and when she comes back, she has another glass of water. She hands it to the blond woman, who takes it without speaking. Mama crosses her arms and sighs audibly.

"This isn't the first time, this situation with Greta, is it?"

The psychologist drinks all the water in one gulp.

"No. But she's the first one to get pregnant. As far as I know."

So Alex has had other lovers before me. Or maybe even at the same time? Who knows. I look inside myself for some sort of reaction to this fact but find none.

"It was when my mother was in the hospital that I found out about the affair. I heard about the baby later, after my mother . . . after she died."

Mama goes back to the sofa and sits down on one end.

"I'm sorry."

The psychologist twirls the glass in her hand, staring as if it might contain answers.

"He wasn't sorry. Watching other people suffer, hurting them himself, that's the breath of life to Alex. He's good at it, and he does it every way he can. With his words, with his actions, with his hands."

This is her husband she's talking about. My ex-lover. Her words conjure up images in my mind, send shivers through my body. So I'm not alone in experiencing those repeated episodes of pain and humiliation. What has he subjected her to—this woman he's lived with so long? I think of the cardigans and jackets she used to wear when I went to her office. Rarely any bare skin, even though it was summer. Suddenly, I understand.

And yet, the thought races through my mind, *and yet you married him and stayed with him. Why?* The next second, I picture a little fair-haired girl with dimples. And I know why.

"It was worse in the beginning. Before I understood the codes and learned to submit. Nowadays he hardly ever . . ."

The psychologist raises her arm and clenches her fist, then slowly lowers her arm again to cup her hand over her mouth.

". . . grabs me."

"When did you realize you needed to submit? When did you start believing there was something wrong with you, that you were to blame for the way he treated you?"

At first, I think I've misunderstood. Surely Mama can't be the one saying things like that. I turn to stare at her, but she isn't looking at me. She seems to be calmly straightening her clothes, smoothing imaginary wrinkles. And the psychologist reacts. The hand clasped over her mouth drops to her lap, and she stares at my mother for a long moment. Then her eyes seem to cloud, and her face softens.

"I know exactly," she says. "It was the first time he said . . ."

She stops, pressing a hand to her throat. I see the gold ring on her left hand. I see how she's trembling. Mama leans forward and tilts her head to one side. Her voice is gentle.

"What did he say?"

"*You're sick in the head. Fucking sick. Something is all twisted up in there.* I don't remember exactly when or where, or what I had done to annoy him that time. But I do remember how it felt when he said that. The words shot right through me, silencing me. I walked around all day in a daze. Everyone I met, the woman standing in front of me in line at the grocery store, the father who picked up his child at the same time I did from preschool . . . *Today my husband said I'm sick in the head. What do you think about that?* That's what I wanted to ask them. But of course, I didn't."

I see Alex's grinning face in front of me. Hear the words he spoke. *I think you're a little crazy. Not exactly right in the head.*

Supporting herself on the arm of the chair, the psychologist slowly gets to her feet.

"That night, when I laid my head on my pillow, I finally understood why those particular words hit me so hard. Why I fell silent instead of defending myself. What he'd said . . . That wasn't some accusation grabbed out of thin air, not some dumb insult. I've never been . . . have never felt entirely . . ."

Standing there, she aims a small kick at the stack of newspapers and pieces of wood, scattering them across the rug. Then she takes off her white sweater and runs her hands up and down her pale arms.

"Deep inside, I knew he was right. What he said was true."

She shifts position, resting her weight on one leg. The blue fabric of her dress clings to her body, revealing a flat stomach and jutting hip bones. In spite of the heat, she wears her blond hair loose, the strands framing her face. She has no makeup on. We couldn't be more different. Or more alike.

"So that was the moment I understood. I knew that no one else would ever put up with me. Since then, he's done his best to remind me that without him I'm nothing. And I . . . Well, I've done what I can to . . . cooperate."

The psychologist turns so the sun streaming in the window lights up her left arm and cheek.

Mama's face is a mask of grim resolve.

"Until now," she says, managing to make it sound like a statement and a question at the same time.

The psychologist looks at her. Then her gaze shifts to the edge of the rug and the bulge over the ax handle. She looks at Mama again.

"Exactly," she says hesitantly. "Until now."

I sense a certain bewilderment in her. And I wonder what is going to happen next. Where do we go from here? Where can we go? Then I don't have time to think or feel anymore. Because at that second, there's a knock on the door.

41

Someone gasps. Mama and the psychologist exchange quick glances. Nobody moves. Another knock, harder and more demanding this time. Mama is finally the one who gets up. She smooths her hair and, moving stiffly, goes out to the entryway.

When she comes back, two police officers are accompanying her. One is the woman I talked to the other day. She glances around the room, noting the torn-up newspapers and the demolished coffee table. She looks at me lying on the floor, then at Mama and the blond woman in the blue dress, and then back at me.

"What's going on here?"

When I don't reply, she turns to her colleague, a man with a receding hairline and a huge paunch. He puts his hands on his hips as he steps forward.

"We had a call from an elderly man. Something about an ax. A woman here in the neighborhood whose behavior seemed confused and threatening. Can you tell us anything about that?"

Something about an ax. I have to make an effort not to look at the bulge in the rug. Out of the corner of my eye, I see the psychologist retreat, taking such small steps that it barely looks like she's moving. She's now standing very close to the ax. Is she trying to use her body to hide the ax? Or is she preparing to grab the concealed weapon and take us all by surprise, if necessary? I force myself not to turn in her direction. Instead, I fix my eyes on the female police officer.

"The old man was out walking his dog when he ran into the woman," she says. "He told us that she was incoherent and seemed extremely upset. And she was carrying an ax, as my colleague just mentioned. So we're taking a look around the neighborhood. It's pretty deserted, but we're knocking on doors to find out if anyone has seen anything suspicious."

Again, she looks around the room, then at each of us in turn. No one responds. Mama's eyes keep shifting, narrowing as she thinks. It occurs to me that she doesn't know I'm the woman the police are talking about, that the ax was originally mine. She's only seen it in the hands of the blond woman. What's going through her mind right now? Will she accuse the psychologist? Is she considering telling the police what's really been going on here?

Part of me is screaming at her to do it, to save us both while she can. Another part of me is still acutely aware that the psychologist is within arm's reach of the ax. If she wanted, she could split my head in half before the officers reacted. If the situation got desperate enough.

Mama opens her mouth to speak, but then closes it again, shaking her head. The male police officer wipes his forehead and loudly clears his throat.

"Well, you're certainly a lively and talkative bunch."

"What exactly happened here?" says his colleague.

She casts another critical glance around the room before her eyes stop on me. She comes a few steps closer, tilts her head to one side, and squints down at me. I fight off an impulse to close my eyes and turn away. Instead, I steel myself and meet her gaze. I'm waiting for her to recognize me, to remember my irrational behavior the last time we met. But maybe because there are other people in the room, or maybe because she really doesn't recognize me with no makeup and in my current state, the only thing she says is:

"How did you get those cuts on your face? And that bruise?"

Mama steps forward so she's standing between me and the officers.

"As you can see, my daughter isn't well. She's just escaped an abusive relationship. And to make matters worse, she's running a fever. You can feel her forehead for yourselves, if you like. I've been with her all day, and she's been in no condition to go anywhere since—"

"All day, you say?"

The policewoman straightens her back, fixing her eyes on my mother. The air is thick with tension. Something is clearly hanging in the balance. Mama seems to have recovered from her initial paralysis. With an unwavering gaze, she meets the eye of the female officer, who, after a moment, utters what sounds like a sigh of resignation. Then she turns to her colleague and raises one eyebrow.

"Well, who knows?" he says with a shrug. "Nobody seems to have seen this ax lady other than an elderly man walking his dog."

He raises his hands to sketch quote marks in the air around the words *ax lady*. The gesture, combined with the expression on his beefy face, indicates he's not sure how much credence to give to the claims of a lonely old man.

The dark-haired female officer again turns to me, and this time I can clearly see that she recognizes me. She stares for a long moment. Her lips are pursed into a thin line.

"If someone has been hurting you, you should file a report," she says at last. "There's help available."

She gestures toward the shattered table behind us. Maybe she thinks it's a result of the violent relationship Mama alluded to.

"Take care of yourself, okay?" she adds.

Without waiting for a reply, she turns to face my mother, who nods emphatically.

"I'll make sure she gets the best possible care."

The officer stifles a sigh.

"Abusive relationships seem to be the theme of the day. We had another complaint earlier. A worried mother whose daughter was purportedly threatened with a knife by her boyfriend. I don't suppose you've—?"

Before she can finish her sentence, the male officer takes a step forward.

"It's a kid we've had our eye on for a while. The leader of some sort of gang that seems to specialize in mistreating animals."

A hint of annoyance in the policewoman's eyes reveals that she thinks it unnecessary for her colleague to give such a detailed explanation. I feel a hard knot form in my stomach. Mistreating animals? Wielding a knife? The girl, Greta. I want to shout, *Is she okay?* But the words fail to come out. In spite of the water I drank, my throat again feels parched. Mama puts her hand to her chest and takes a deep breath.

"Oh, my God. How terrible! That poor girl! And mistreating animals? What on earth for?"

Something black-and-white streaks past in my mind. I can almost feel an agile little body curl up next to me. Then the image dissolves, and the feeling of warmth fades, to be replaced by something sharp and cold. *Tirith.*

"Who knows?" says the policeman with a shrug. "Maybe they're sadists. Or maybe they're just bored. Kids these days—"

"Anyway," says the female officer, cutting him off. "We're not going to stand here speculating. But if you've seen or heard anything that might help us with the case . . ."

Mama shakes her head. Her face is pale.

"No. Thank God we just happen to be here on a short visit. And considering all the awful things that seem to be happening around here, I don't think we'll be back. Malice. What kind of name is that for a lake?"

The policewoman raises her hands, palms up.

"It's not the official name. But I guess it is a little off-putting. Not exactly the kind of name that attracts tourists. But I'm new here. It was only a few days ago I heard that's what the locals call the lake."

And with that, she turns and takes a few steps toward the front entryway. Are they leaving? Already? Anxiously, I shift position, unable to decide whether I'm more afraid of having the police here or seeing them leave. I think about the black object hidden under the rug. The big mess in the room must have distracted the officers from noticing the bulge.

The male officer is already out in the hall when the policewoman pauses. She turns to look at the psychologist. And the corner of the rug. I hold my breath. Follow the officer's gaze. I see Alex's wife, Smilla's mother, standing there in her blue dress, leaning against the wall as if she wishes she could disappear into it.

"And you? Who are you?"

The psychologist hesitates, doesn't speak. I seem to see her slide down the wall, and I imagine her reaching out a trembling hand toward the floor. It might be real; it might be my imagination. *Yes, who are you?* That's the question that races through my battered mind. Then I hear a familiar voice answer.

"A friend," says Mama. "She's a friend."

I see the police officer turn back to look at my mother. Maybe Mama hesitated a second too long. But when she did speak, there wasn't a trace of doubt in her voice. Now she nods to underscore her words. A friend. Yes. They look at each other. And I have a feeling my mother protecting the psychologist from the police isn't only about me. There's something else.

Both officers are now out in the front hall. I hear the door close after them. My mother and the psychologist study each other for a long moment. Mama breaks the silence.

"All right then. Give me the ax, and I'll put it away. Then we'll sit down and talk. You can ask me anything you like. I can tell you want to know."

Both Mama and the psychologist move slowly. I watch as something black is picked up and changes hands. I hear footsteps leaving the room, a door opening, a clattering sound, and then the footsteps come back. No more sounds after that, except for voices, speaking quietly. A rushing inside my head. My eyes fall shut. I'm tired. So terribly tired.

42

I fall asleep and dream that Mama and my former psychologist are sitting across from me, at either end of the sofa, talking. And that, every once in a while, Mama leans forward to feel my forehead or straighten the pillow she has slipped under my head. In my dream, I hear the psychologist say: *So your friend was in love with your husband? Was that why she told him about the slap? To make him leave you?*

"Or else they were already having an affair," I hear my mother say, and then I realize that I'm awake. "Maybe she felt rejected since he was continuing to see other women. Who knows?"

There is no bitterness or hatred in her voice when she talks about Ruth. It sounds more like she's tired. At first I find this surprising. Then I think it's strange I would have this reaction. Because what is the basis for my perception of my mother's feelings or her view of what happened? I have never—never ever—curled up on the sofa beside her to discuss these things. Neither of us has ever made any serious attempt to initiate that kind of conversation. Mama may have tried when I was a teenager, but I brushed all her efforts aside. Then I moved away from home and withdrew even more, keeping my distance. And now we've ended up here.

They think I'm still asleep, and I let them, lying still and opening my eyes only a little bit. In the center of my field of vision, right in front of me, is a pair of slender legs. Not Mama's. The sunlight streaming into the room falls in such a way that I can clearly see the unshaven hair on her calves. One foot is bobbing up and down, wearing a loose-fitting sandal. I see the peeling nail polish, some sort of hopeless pastel color. She's sitting so close that I could reach out my hand and touch her. Caress her leg. Or scratch it.

"I have to ask . . . Afterward . . . Wasn't there anyone who . . . I mean . . ."

The fact that she's having such trouble saying the words makes me realize what she wants to know. Mama understands too. Of course.

"It was declared an accident. The neighbors in the apartments above and below had heard a man bellowing a while earlier and thought it must be the same man who came home late, making a lot of noise in the stairwell. The people who lived across the street told the police they'd seen the man smoking in the open window lots of times. They'd wondered how he dared, since he lived on such a high floor. The autopsy found alcohol in his blood, quite a lot. I think they even found pieces of the glass he'd been holding—"

I move abruptly, kicking out my leg so they can't miss seeing it. Mama stops at once. Her face peers down at me from the sofa.

"Hello there. You fell asleep, and I decided not to wake you. Thought you could use a rest. I would have moved you, but . . . Well, you're a little bigger now than the last time I carried you to bed."

We look at each other. For a long moment. Until Mama blushes. She really does. She blushes, though only briefly. Then she hurries to regain control of the situation.

"How are you feeling?"

Even though I've been awake for several minutes, it's only when I hear her question that I take stock. My head is no longer pounding fiercely. The headache is still there, but not as sharp. My shoulder still feels stiff and swollen, but the fever must have subsided. The nap seems to have done me good. How long did I sleep? A familiar, and yet peculiar, feeling starts up in my stomach.

"Hungry," I say. "I'm hungry."

I go out to the kitchen, walking with my mother's arm around me for support, and there I eat several pieces of toast. I wonder what happened to the ax. I wonder what Mama has done with it, but I don't ask. Smilla's baby doll is lying facedown on the floor under the table. Her polka-dot dress has slid up so that the doll's shiny plastic bottom peeks out. Slowly but deliberately, I reach for the doll, straighten her clothes, and set her on the chair next to me.

The effort prompts my bad shoulder to throb with pain. The lower part of my face and my neck hurt. I'm still exhausted, both from the fever and from the havoc of the past few days. Anxiously, I run my fingertips over the skin around my navel. *Are you still in there?* Deep inside, I feel something flutter. Something that's fighting. Something that wants to live. Something or someone. It's going to be fine. It has to be.

With my newly awakened appetite, I set about filling the gaping hole in my stomach while my mother rummages around in the bedroom and bathroom, packing up all my things. She works efficiently, in silence, moving with confidence, as if she's never done anything other than rescue me from absurd situations. I'm guessing that her plan is to finish up as soon as possible and then drive me to the hospital. I wonder what she's going to tell the doctors. It's probably best not to ask, best for me to keep quiet and let Mama do the talking.

The psychologist stays out of our way, but I know she hasn't left the cabin. Her presence is palpable. I assume she's still in the living room.

Pondering her next step, pondering her life? What do I know? The only thing I know is that if Mama trusts her, then I trust her too.

I've finally eaten my fill. Mama has wiped off the kitchen counter and carried out my suitcase.

"The car is parked outside," she says, motioning toward the front door.

Then she helps me up, and we start walking, her arm around my waist, my arm around her neck. Our bodies pressed together from shoulder to hip. We haven't stood this close in a long time.

We're already out on the front steps when I hear a sound from the hall. Mama turns her head, her eyes fixed on something right behind us.

"I have one last question. Was it worth it?"

Mama hesitates. She looks from the psychologist to me, her gaze lingering on me for a moment. I don't turn around. I don't meet my mother's eye. I'm waiting.

"No," says Mama. "It wasn't."

She steers me toward her car and helps me into the passenger seat. Through the window, I see my own car. I half listen as Mama tells me she's going to have it towed from here as soon as possible. She'll figure it out. I shouldn't worry. I won't need to come back here. Ever. She'll see to that.

She walks around the car and gets into the driver's seat, closing the door and fastening her seatbelt. Then she sits there without turning the key. She doesn't move. She doesn't say anything.

"Mama?"

For a long time, she stares straight ahead.

"That man . . . Alex," she finally says. "The way he treats her . . . Does he treat you like that too?"

What should I say? Should I tell her about the silk tie? Mama is chewing her lip. I try to sound reassuring, convincing.

"I left him. I told him never to come near me again."

She thinks about this for a moment.

"What about the child?" she says then. "Your child. What are you planning to do?"

I wait, forcing her to turn toward me and read the answer in my eyes. Slowly, she nods. She reaches out her hand and cups my unbruised cheek.

"If he ever contacts you—you or the baby—if he in any way . . ."

Sooner or later, Alex is going to find out that I got away, that his wife let me go. How will he react? I don't want to even try imagining that. But no matter how strong his reaction, he'll probably think twice before contacting me again. There are certain advantages to being a mystery. There are certain advantages to not telling Alex the whole truth about Papa.

I think about what he said to me at the end of our latest—our last—phone conversation. And about what I let him believe. That I was the one who delivered the fatal shove on that night an eternity ago. What I'm capable of.

I raise my hand to place it over my mother's hand on my cheek. I hope she'll know what I'm trying to say. I hope she can feel the strength of who I am. *My mother's daughter.*

"If he does, I'll deal with it."

Mama listens, lets the words sink in. Then she removes her hand and smiles. That smile tells me that everything is as it should be.

"Wait here a minute," she says. "I forgot something inside."

She unbuckles her seatbelt and resolutely walks around the hedge that encloses the cabin we're about to leave.

I lean back and take several deep breaths. *Leaving this place. At last.* I think about how good it will be to go home. I decide to look for a new apartment as soon as possible. Somewhere he's never been. Maybe I'll even move to a different town. But the very first thing I'm going to do, as soon as I've gotten patched up and I'm feeling better, is call Katinka. And ask her if she'd like to meet for coffee.

At that moment, I see her. She's approaching hesitantly from the other side of the road. Black, shapeless clothes, her long hair hanging loose. I open the car door, and she comes over, stopping a few feet away. She stares at me mutely, her eyes shifting from the cuts on my face to the big bruise.

"My mom talked to the police," she says at last. "They said something about a woman with an ax. I wanted . . . I just wanted to see if you were okay."

"I'm okay. What about you?"

She brushes her hair out of her face and stares down at the ground. *A worried mother whose daughter was purportedly threatened with a knife by her boyfriend.* That's what the police officer had said.

"Your mother reported him?"

The girl named Greta looks at the ground, at the road, everywhere but at me.

"So fucking stupid," she finally mutters. "She has no idea what she's talking about."

I have a sinking feeling in my chest. So she's taking Jorma's side? Even though he tried to attack her? I want to shake her, protest, ask her if she heard anything I said when we met in the forest clearing. But then I glimpse my mother coming around the hedge. When she catches sight of Greta, she walks faster. Quickly, I reach out my hand and hear the words of the policewoman echoing from my own lips.

"There's help available."

The girl looks at my hand held out toward her. For a moment, she doesn't move. Then she raises her own hand and her fingers brush mine. They're ice cold.

"Hello there. Who are you? And what are you doing here?"

Mama's voice is loud and commanding. The girl yanks her hand away. She looks into my eyes one last time. My voice is barely more than a whisper.

"Take care of yourself, okay?"

Without another word, she runs off. I feel my own hand fall away. Mama opens the car door, gets in, and fastens her seatbelt. When she asks me about the girl, I shrug. She doesn't persist.

"Sweetheart," she says instead, "there's something I was thinking about."

I close the car door and look in the mirror. I see a small, thin figure disappearing. Soon, she's no more than a line in the distance. Then she's swallowed up by the earth. By Marhem. Mama turns the key, and the engine starts up.

"I hope you know that I'd do anything for you. Anything at all, Greta."

I nod. I do know.

"You're going to need a lot of help. It's no easy thing to be pregnant. And later, after the baby arrives, it won't exactly get easier. As a single mother, you'll need all the support you can get. I want you to know that I . . ."

She comes to a halt. I fumble for her hand resting on the gearshift.

"Mama. Thank you."

She turns to look at me and smiles. That special smile of hers.

Then we drive off.

43

I didn't manage to strike a good blow with the oar. The angle was wrong, the force of the blow too weak. You passed out, but that was mostly due to the already-pitiful condition you were in. Maybe I should have used the ax while you were lying on the floor. Before she arrived. The person who turned everything upside down. Your mother.

I recognized you as soon as you opened the door, knew that you were a former client, but it took a while before I was able to place you. Then I remembered the strange story about your father falling out the window. The story that never had a proper ending. I was so sure, back then when you sat across from me and talked around the issue. I was sure that you were the one who pushed him. Everything about you—your body language, your tone, your facial expressions—indicated as much. So when you wanted to end our meetings without fully unburdening your heart, I tried to stop you. Do you remember that? You probably don't. My words can't have meant much to you. You left my office and never came back. And I moved on too. I haven't given you a thought since that day. Not until now.

I stand in the kitchen and look out the window. Even though I can't see you, I know you're still out there. A moment ago, I heard a car door slam.

In a few seconds, the engine will start up, and I'll stand here listening as you and your mother disappear. Will I have any regrets then? Will I regret that I let you go, that I didn't use my bare hands to yank out of you what is growing inside?

It's for your mother's sake that I'm letting you go. After she shared her story with me, I can't lift a hand to her daughter. I thought I'd already been through the worst, but now I have a feeling something even bigger is just around the corner. Something both frightening and powerful. The biggest challenge of my life. Something that will set me free.

I see her running back toward the cabin, hear her feet pounding up the steps, and then the front door opens. You must have forgotten something. I go out to the hall to meet her. She doesn't take off her shoes, doesn't make any move to come inside. She just stands there, staring at me.

"Greta won't have anything more to do with your husband," she says at last. "You have my word."

I know she wouldn't say that if it wasn't true. I've seen with my own eyes the power she has over you. You may not see it yourself. Maybe you don't want to admit it, but that's how it is. I nod to show that I accept her message. I expect her to turn and leave. But she stays where she is, standing on the hall rug.

"You asked me if it was worth it. Ask me again."

At first, I'm confused. She already answered my question. Then I understand. You're not here listening this time. I feel my pulse quicken.

"Was it worth it?"

"I've finally asked Greta to forgive me for leaving her alone. It's been weighing on me all these years. But what I did, the fact that I killed her father, that's not something I've asked her to forgive. And I'm never going to insult her or myself by doing that. A genuine plea for forgiveness presupposes remorse."

Her words swirl through the air between us. She locks her eyes on mine, boring into me.

"Is that answer clear enough for you?"

My skin tingles and aches. It feels like every blood vessel in my body is open. I nod. Her words have made something come alive. The big challenge in front of me, awaiting me. I've been brooding about it all afternoon, ever since she finished telling her story. Ever since I heard myself say things about Alex that I'd never said before, expressing myself in a way I never thought possible. And now I understand. It's when I'm with him—not without him—that I'm nothing. So simple, so banal. Yet it's been true this whole time.

I look with astonishment and gratitude at the woman standing in front of me. Finally, I understand the meaning of this seemingly chance meeting here in Marhem.

"I'm sorry about your mother. Were you close?"

I feel a stab of pain in my heart.

"I miss her so much."

She nods briefly and is just about to open the door when she stops. She leans toward me, so close that one of her curls brushes against my temple.

"Make sure your daughter is somewhere else," she whispers. "And make it look like an accident."

Then she's gone. A minute later, I hear the car start, pick up speed, and finally fade into the distance. I stand in the hall, frozen in place. Everything I thought was lost—what I thought had vanished in the chasm opened by my mother's last breath—all of that I can rediscover. All of that I'm going to reclaim. Myself. My daughter. Our future.

A mother's love is boundless, wild, and beautiful. I will honor my mother's memory and continue to strive for the same goals she did. But my path will be different from the one she took. While she chose submission, I choose to fight. Where she chose gentleness, I choose determination. Slowly, I turn around and go back to the living room. I have a lot to think about before I go home. A lot to plan. I sit down on the sofa, the side where your mother was sitting. If I close my eyes, I can still feel the presence of her story.

It gives me both solace and strength. I know that I can make it through this. If she could, I can.

I picture Smilla, hear her infectious laughter ringing in my ears. Sometime, many years from now, maybe we'll sit down and talk. A mother and her grown daughter. Then I'll tell her about my path through life, about the lessons I've learned. I don't yet know exactly what I'll say. But I do know where I'll begin. I know what the first sentence of my story will be:

A good mother is not shaped by circumstances. She is the one who decides how to shape them.

ACKNOWLEDGMENTS

My thanks to my diligent publisher, my insightful first readers, my wonderful friends, and my whole supportive and loving family.

Last but not least, I thank you for reading my book.

ABOUT THE AUTHOR

Photo © 2015

Caroline Eriksson holds a master's degree in social psychology and worked for more than ten years in human-resource management before deciding to pursue writing, her childhood dream. Her first two novels are based on historical Swedish murder cases, and her debut, *The Devil Helped Me*, was nominated for *Stora Ljudbokspriset* (the Big Audiobook Prize) in 2014.

Caroline has lived all over the world. She attended high school in Quantico, Virginia; studied at the University of Adelaide in Australia; and now lives in Stockholm. She denies being a daredevil but admits that she once threw herself off a mountain in New Zealand in a hang-gliding experiment.

Her greatest adventure today is raising her two children, and she satisfies any residual wanderlust by exploring the most terrifying parts of life—its dark psychological elements—in her writing. *The Missing* is Caroline's first psychological suspense thriller and her first book translated into English. She's already hard at work on her next novel.

ABOUT THE TRANSLATOR

Photo © 2007 Steven T. Murray

Tiina Nunnally has translated over sixty works of fiction from Danish, Norwegian, and Swedish. She has received numerous awards for her work, including the PEN/ Book-of-the-Month Club Translation Prize and the Independent Foreign Fiction Prize. The Swedish Academy has honored her for her contributions to "the introduction of Swedish culture abroad." And she was appointed Knight of the Royal Norwegian Order of Merit for her efforts on behalf of Norwegian literature in the United States. Nunnally makes her living as a full-time literary translator.